"I Want You,"

James stated in a deep voice.

"And I you," Isis replied.

"Are you sure, Isis? Once you give yourself to me, once we share ourselves, there'll be no going back."

"I live by my instincts. Time has never had any meaning for me. I don't measure my knowledge by the ticks of a clock or days on a calendar."

"What if there were something you didn't know about me? Something I couldn't tell you?"

Her fingers traced lightly over his features, noting his tense stillness.

"Mind reading?" he probed.

"No. Never with you unless you ask me to. You, more than anyone, are safe from that. I'd never use you that way."

James inhaled sharply at her solemnly given promise. With her very generosity, she was making herself vulnerable to him.

Dear Reader,

Welcome to Silhouette! Our goal is to give you hours of unbeatable reading pleasure, and we hope you'll enjoy each month's six new Silhouette Desires. These sensual, provocative love stories are both believable and compelling—sometimes they're poignant, sometimes humorous, but always enjoyable.

Indulge yourself. Experience all the passion and excitement of falling in love along with our heroine as she meets the irresistible man of her dreams and together they overcome all obstacles in the path to a happy ending.

If this is your first Desire, I hope it'll be the first of many. If you're already a Silhouette Desire reader, thanks for your support! Look for some of your favorite authors in the coming months: Stephanie James, Diana Palmer, Dixie Browning, Ann Major and Doreen Owens Malek, to name just a few.

Happy reading!

Isabel Swift
Senior Editor

SDRL-7/85

SARA CHANCE
Look Beyond Tomorrow

Silhouette Desire
Published by Silhouette Books New York
America's Publisher of Contemporary Romance

SILHOUETTE BOOKS
300 E. 42nd St., New York, N.Y. 10017

Copyright © 1985 by Sydney Ann Clary

Distributed by Pocket Books

ISBN: 0-373-05244-8

First Silhouette Books printing November 1985

10 9 8 7 6 5 4 3 2 1

America's Publisher of Contemporary Romance

Printed in the U.S.A.

Books by Sara Chance

Silhouette Desire

Her Golden Eyes #46
Home at Last #83
This Wildfire Magic #107
A Touch of Passion #183
Look Beyond Tomorrow #244

SARA CHANCE,
"wife, mother, author, in that order," currently resides in Florida with her husband. With the ocean minutes from her door, Ms. Chance enjoys both swimming and boating.

For Isabel, my first editor.
You have taught me so much.
Thank you.

What emptiness I see beyond tomorrow
Lonely is my soul for one who waits for me
Then he comes to fill my life and
All I see beyond tomorrow is our love.

One

Isis closed her sapphire eyes as she breathed in slowly and deeply. Focusing on the inner voice only she could hear, she consciously shut out the sounds of the waiting audience and the emcee's preliminary warm-up before her act. She felt her mental energy rise to meet the demands she would make on it during the next hour. Her thick black lashes lifted the moment she reached her peak of directed concentration just in time to hear the announcer begin her intro.

"Ladies and gentlemen, we are proud to offer you a uniquely talented lady. A woman gifted with the rare power to read minds. No thought is beyond her divining, no wish secret." Near Eastern music filled the air as the lights dimmed to bathe the stage in a soft blue glow. "The Midnight Star presents the goddess Isis, daughter of the Nile."

The curtain rose slowly, cuing Isis. She glided onto the stage, her brief white Egyptian gown with its silver key design flowing around her tall figure. Long legs flashed beneath the transparently thin skirt, drawing every male eye in the silent crowd. The stage lights caught her silver-glitter makeup and the platinum chains at her throat with sparks of cerulean. She paused a moment, arms uplifted, her head thrown back in an attitude of supplication to a higher power. She held her pose, judging to that magic split second of total audience attention. Then she lowered her hands in a graceful arc, her dark eyes scanning the rapt, silent faces before her.

A good crowd, she decided, noting the subtle body movements and facial expression that played a part in her performance. Thoughts assailed her receptive mind as she carefully chose her first subject. She focused on the petite blonde sitting in the first row beside a young, very personable man.

"Honeymoon-newlyweds," she pronounced. The telltale start of surprise from her subject confirmed her accuracy. "Shall I read your mind or his?" She smiled slightly, knowing the gesture lent an air of mystery to her high cheekbones and exotically slanted eyes. She glanced at the husband, allowing her lips to curve more fully on seeing the distinctly male gleam in his eyes. "In any other state but Nevada you'd get arrested for what you're thinking," she pointed out.

Appreciative laughter signaled her listeners' willingness to be entertained. Moving slowly, seemingly at random, Isis worked her way from table to table. A dramatic pause here, a hint of mystery there, thoughts revealed with uncanny accuracy, all these were elements of the act that had made her nationally famous.

As she skillfully led her receptive audience toward the climax of the evening, she reached the group of guests she intended as her finale.

Her eyes beneath their ebony lashes gazed slowly around the small reserved area set aside for the owners of the club or visiting VIPs. Burt Metcalf, a silent partner in the Midnight Star, occupied the center booth with his wife and another couple. Deciding to use Mrs. Metcalf, an avid fan and believer in the paranormal, as her final subject, Isis smiled and announced her intentions. Briefly she let her glance wander over the crowded room, lingering for a split second on the lone male seated just to the left of the Metcalf party.

For three nights she had done her shows, and each time his position was the same. A flicker of unease disturbed her concentration for a moment. The man bothered her with his inattention in spite of his apparently engrossed appearance. He came, but he didn't see or hear her, of that she was certain. Instead, he seemed to focus on someone else. But who?

Suddenly realizing she was hesitating too long, Isis went back to work. With practiced ease, she drew out her eager, interested subject, and in return she mentally lifted Buffy Metcalf's answers to her spoken questions. The resulting thunder of applause when she finished was satisfyingly long. Isis mounted the stage once more to take a final bow.

As she raised her head, her eyes caught that man's. It was the first time in three nights that he had looked directly at her, she realized in surprise.

Metcalf! The name flashed across her tired mind. Sapphires! Diamonds! Steal! She stepped back automatically while on cue the curtain began its descent. She shook her head as the velvet barrier shielded her from the audience's sight. A thief? Here? She shrugged her idea away, for once refusing to acknowledge her inner voice. She wasn't sure why she felt the need to discount her usually reliable gift, but she did.

"You were great, Miss O'Shea," one of the scantily clad dancers of the next act whispered as she passed Isis.

Isis smiled with a pleasantly voiced word of thanks. Skirting the various people and backstage equipment, she made her way wearily to her dressing room. "One more night," she said with a sigh as she entered to find her dresser waiting for her. "This tour has been a killer."

"I don't know what your agent was thinking of, booking you like that," Josie scolded, helping Isis out of her costume to leave her attired in a brief flesh-colored teddy. "I swear I barely had a chance to find my toothbrush before we were moving again. Three months on the road."

Obeying the pressure of the older woman's hand on her shoulder, Isis sank down in the chair before the brightly lit makeup table. "Max was only doing his job. Besides, I'm the one who agreed."

Josie glared at her in the mirror while her nimble fingers released the high plaited crown of midnight hair. "And look at you. You've lost ten pounds and you've got shadows under your eyes," she pointed out tartly. She brushed the long mat black mane until it lay in a midnight swathe against Isis's bare back.

Isis stared at her reflection, knowing her friend was right. She really shouldn't have agreed to so long a tour. The strain had been far greater than she had antici- pated. She was exhausted clear through to her bones. Even the pins Josie used to secure her hairstyle seemed to hurt her. She wanted to sleep but knew she wouldn't. At least not until she wound down a little.

"I think I'll walk through the casino for a while," she murmured as Josie cleansed her face.

"What?" she all but shrieked. "You're not serious!"

Isis nodded, giving her companion a faintly pleading look. "Only for an hour, I promise." As she spoke she started to reapply her makeup, only slightly toning down the exotic aura of her stage appearance.

"I'm going to come after you if you don't keep your word," Josie threatened.

"Fair enough." Isis grinned, knowing Josie was voicing her concern in the only way she could. She rose and strolled to the closet. The flamboyant array of colors her many costumes had was echoed in the raw silk rainbow-hued evening caftan she selected to wear from her everyday wardrobe. The delicate fabric floated over her curves in whispery drapes, creating a vibrant, yet elusive, image.

"Shall I put your hair up again?"

Isis grimaced. "No, my head aches as it is. I'd rather leave it down," she replied, slipping her feet into the silver ribbon heels that complemented her gown. She bent slightly to give Josie a quick hug. "Don't scowl at me. It'll give you wrinkles."

"If you knew what I was thinking, you wouldn't tease me," Josie retorted, her brown eyes gleaming with annoyance.

Isis grinned, unabashed at her comment. "You know I make it a policy not to 'peep' into my friends' minds," she pointed out meekly. She accepted the small clutch bag Josie handed her, one eyebrow winging wickedly upward. Sapphire eyes, the deep dark blue of Lake Tahoe, reflected her amusement at Josie's blatantly obvious chagrin.

"Out," the other woman commanded with mock ferocity.

Isis laughed softly as the dressing-room door snapped shut behind her. It had only been five years since Ned and Josie Sullivan had entered her life, yet in many ways it seemed as if the older couple were the family she no longer had. Josie was her dresser, friend, companion and confidante when she was on tour, while Ned was the caretaker of her small estate, Moonlight Oasis, on the California-Nevada side of Lake Tahoe. When Isis was in residence, Josie took her place as housekeeper, jealously guarding her home and privacy with all the zeal of an abbess in a nunnery.

Soon she and Josie would return there to rest for the winter. Ned would be happy to have his wife back, Josie would be happy to finally unpack her suitcase, while Isis would be happy to...To what, she asked herself as she crossed the crowded gambling room. The clink of dice, the whispered incantations from pleading gamblers formed a strange background for her thoughts. She had everything she wanted now that Oasis was finished and her career was expanding. She must be more weary than she supposed, she decided on recognizing a vague, unexplained emptiness within her.

Halting at the edge of a small crowd gathered around the blackjack table, Isis idly watched the play of emotions over the engrossed faces. A squeal of delight drew her gaze to the white-haired woman on the middle stool. She recognized Buffy Metcalf immediately, even without the ever-present shadow of her husband's stocky form.

"Are you going to play or watch?"

At the sound of the quietly spoken question, Isis turned to find herself staring into the calm hazel eyes of the strange man in the audience.

"I beg your pardon," she murmured automatically. "Where you speaking to me?"

He inclined his head once, then restated his query in the same gentle, even tone he had used before.

Isis studied him, making no secret of her interest. "I'm watching," she replied while concentrating on his thoughts. Oddly, there was no discernible pattern. A random word or two with more feeling than definitive ideas. Curiosity, intrigue and reserve. But most of all power. Power? She frowned, examining the unexpected sensation.

"Will you have a drink with me?"

Isis refocused on her questioner. "Why?" she responded bluntly, catching the slight flicker of his lashes.

"Why not?" He smiled faintly. "I'm very respectable, I assure you." He touched her arm lightly. "There's a nice corner in the lounge where we can talk," he explained easily. "Will you come?"

Isis looked down at his hand, then back to his face. Why was she hesitating? Normally she would have politely declined, yet something stopped her. In her business she knew how to distinguish a kook from a nice human being. This man was no weirdo. He had a direct gaze that was neither blatantly hungry nor disappointingly unappreciative. His medium brown hair and ordinary hazel eyes matched his trim yet uninspiring body. The sport jacket and tamely toned slacks he wore reflected a middle-class conservatism that was pleasing if not exciting.

"All right," she agreed finally with a light professional smile. Instinct prompted her acceptance, that much she knew and recognized. But she still didn't know why. "You know my name, but I don't know yours," she added as she walked beside him. Privately she was amazed at how well their strides seemed to match. Being a tall woman, she was accustomed to dwarfing most of the men she knew. But not this one. In spite of the fact he probably was only an inch or two taller than she was.

"James Leland."

Once again the liquid smooth voice invaded her thoughts, startling her. "Do you go by Jim or Jimmy?" she asked conversationally. She took the seat he held for her.

"James."

One brow quirked at the brief reply, silently expressing her curiosity as she watched him settle into his place across the small table. He should have been Jim or maybe even Jimmy to fit the image he projected. Why the formal, more forceful James?

"Can you really read minds or—" He paused, politely allowing his unfinished sentence to speak for itself.

"Or is it a glitzy flash trick?" She lifted her chin in an unconscious gesture of pride. Somehow she had not expected him to be a skeptic. After all, he had sat through three of her shows. Certainly that alone argued more than a passing interest.

"I didn't mean to make you angry," he apologized swiftly, reaching out to cover her hand with his. The last thing he wanted was to annoy her. She was his ticket to Metcalf's south shore estate. He had to have the entry her fame, beauty and expertise granted her if he was to succeed.

"Just exactly what are you after, James?" she asked, withdrawing from his grasp with careful precision. "You've been at my show since I opened here, but I don't think you're a fan."

James stiffened, alert to the danger of trying to deceive this woman. If she had only a portion of the ability she was reported to possess, she would discover his motive. "Not a fan, exactly," he admitted slowly as though reluctant to confess his reasons. He tried the hesitant, half-shy smile that usually disarmed the unwary, without any measurable success. Perhaps flattery would distract her. "I've always been curious about the paranormal. Since I was vacationing here, I decided to see your performance. You have quite a reputation, you know, especially after that article in the Aspen paper about you."

Isis heard his words, yet it was his expression and the barely perceptible stillness of his body to which she listened. She was too drained mentally to attempt to read him with any degree of accuracy.

"You have done your research well," she observed, studying him closely.

James shrugged slightly, dismissing her comment. "It made the national wire services—psychic finds lost teenager despite blizzard conditions. Anyone would remember you."

His gaze locked on her features. Momentarily, he forgot his role in his appreciation of the unusual composition of her face. Slanted eyes beneath delicate black brows and thick ebony lashes reflected the heritage of her Eurasian mother. The sculpted cheekbones, too, were probably a gift of her mixed ancestry, but the intense blue eyes, the generous mouth and regal height had to be the Irish of her father's people.

"You're very beautiful," he said softly, but with such a lack of emphasis, Isis blinked.

"Not really," she denied, oddly off balance at the sudden intrusion of sexual awareness. For a split second his ordinary hazel eyes had gleamed with molten gold and jade. There was a cloaked strength in his expression that she had missed until this moment. She shook her head as a scant heartbeat later the image dissolved before her eyes, leaving behind a perfectly nice, but unexciting man.

"It's late. I really must go." She rose, conscious of the exhausted limpness stealing over her.

"You're dead on your feet," he murmured, moving to her side to take her arm. "Let me walk you to your room."

Isis met his eyes, searching for a hint of something to object to. But there was nothing. No sexual innuendo, no male interest. Nothing beyond simple concern. She nodded, unable to deny the support he offered. His warm touch conveyed a firm assurance and confidence she found pleasing though contrary to the unassuming image he projected.

He made no effort to speak as he subtly guided her from the lounge to the elevators. Within moments he delivered her to her hotel room, took her key and opened the door for her. He reached inside, flipped on the lights, then turned and handed her the key.

"I meant what I said downstairs. You are very beautiful," he whispered softly, his voice flowing over her in a liquid river of sound.

Isis stared at him, soothed into utter stillness. Once again she was prey to two different sensations. A man behind a man. One was strong, alert, aware; the other quiet, nonassertive, bland. Both couldn't be real. Two such contradictory personalities in the same being were against every law in nature.

"Isis?"

Her name on his lips drew her back to him. She blinked, and the swirling emotional patterns dissipated, leaving her swaying slightly in the aftermath.

James caught her shoulders to steady her. The slender fragility of the bones beneath his fingers surprised him, making him aware of her as a woman. The scent of jasmine and roses wove elusive, fragrant tendrils around him, teasing his senses. The vibrant rainbow silk of the fabric covering her added to her mystique.

"I'm all right, really," she murmured, wriggling slightly in a bid for release.

"Yes." James drew his hands away, more reluctantly than he cared to admit.

He was on a job. He couldn't afford this complication, he assured himself sternly as he stepped back a pace. He stood silently while Isis turned from him and entered her room without a backward look. The door clicked shut, leaving him alone in the empty corridor.

His dossier on Isis O'Shea had prepared him for her psychic abilities and in some measure for her unique presence. But nothing had warned him of the pure male desire heating his blood. What he was feeling could easily spell the ruin of his assignment. Yet, oddly, it could also mark his success as well. He strolled toward the elevator, going over his strategy.

He had intended to attach himself to Isis from the moment he had overheard Metcalf asking her to give a private performance for his Christmas party at his estate. He had to get into the Metcalf home on some innocuous pretext. What could be more innocuous than to attend as Isis's escort?

Of course, such a plan had a number of drawbacks, one being if she was involved with someone. Fortunately, his research had laid that problem to rest. The lady traveled solo. But he still had two major obstacles to surmount—her refusal of the club owner's invitation, and the single day left to him before she left for her home on the northeastern shore of Tahoe.

He entered his room, frowning at the need he had for speed. Time was running out. He had to locate the Sapphire Shower. No matter how much he might wish there were another way to get himself onto Metcalf's home ground, there wasn't. Isis was his only hope beyond the direct approach, which had already failed more than once.

Isis leaned back against the door, her gaze roaming blankly around the sumptuous but impersonal room. She should move, but the waiting presence she sensed on the corridor side of the panel held her in place. Just for a moment, when he had touched her, she had seen desire in his eyes. Was it still there? Was that why he was standing in the hall? She shut her eyes against the fantasy her light-headedness had created. Josie was right, she was past being exhausted; she was wiped out. She pushed herself upright and padded toward her bed, shedding her caftan and teddy with barely a break in her stride. Her shoes were the last to go before she slipped between the cool sheets. Whatever James Leland was, he played no part in her life. He was, quite simply, a pleasant man who had bought her a drink one night.

Two

Isis surfaced from the depths of sleep with the instant alertness of one who has lived most of her early life in primitive surroundings. One by one, she tensed and relaxed her muscles as she lay staring at the muted sunlit patterns on her ceiling. The small exercise, taught to her by her Egyptologist father, restored the suppleness of movement the night's rest had stolen from her body. She rose, casting an absent glance at her travel clock.

A smile lifted the corners of her lips on seeing it was only midafternoon. She had plenty of time to dress and have her breakfast-lunch-dinner before going for her daily walk.

Two hours later she exited the hotel and strolled the short distance down to the lake. She breathed deeply of the clear, crisp air, feeling the residue from her smoky, nightly environment leave her. Her boots crunched softly through the snow as she took the left fork of the path running along the water's edge. Pines reached to the sky in arrow-straight spires above her. Silence surrounded her as the trees absorbed the sounds of the busy streets of the town.

Tahoe in winter was a sportsman's paradise, offering everything from skiing to snow camping. The roads were lined with cars, making travel slow and parking impossible. The motels, lodges and cabins were filled to capacity with avid athletes as well as those who came to enjoy Nevada's favorite indoor sport, gambling.

Yet for her, Tahoe held something beyond the man-made pleasures and pastimes. There was a serenity in this beautiful setting where a sapphire lake lay like a jewel ringed with jagged snow-covered mountains, where evergreens glowed with the richness of emerald and jade against a blinding white winter canvas. Powers surpassing the puny efforts of man had created this majestic land. Here Isis felt more at home than anywhere else in all her travels.

Because of her psychic gift, she had often felt an outcast from her environment and those she met. Even in Egypt, where she had spent almost all her life until her father died when she was seventeen, she had been aware of her uniqueness. College had been a nightmare of adaptations and adjustments, with more to come when she had graduated with a master's in library science. Her flamboyant, colorful clothes and exotic appearance caused innumerable problems in her job. When her mind-reading abilities had become known, she had been politely asked to resign from the library staff.

From that moment on fate had taken a hand. The college job of doing readings for frat and sorority houses had, by a streak of accidental good luck, gotten her an engagement at a small lounge. Max Bauman, an up-and-coming talent agent, had been in the audience and had promptly approached her after her show.

She smiled, remembering her rotund friend's forceful manner and caustic wit. She gazed out across the dark blue lake, mentally thanking whatever chance had brought the two of them together. For it had been Max's astute handling and blunt-spoken support that had eased her way in the tough entertainment world. Now she was in the happy position of being able to pick and choose when she wanted to work.

A sigh gusted from her lips as she leaned back against the rock on which she was sitting. Life was good, she decided, her gaze drinking in the beauty of the dying sun across the mountains and the dark surface of Lake Tahoe. Pink, magenta, gold, orange merged into a vivid display unrivaled by anything man had ever created. The white of the snow was bathed in the glorious overflow of color.

She wrapped her arms around herself, hugging her scarlet parka against her chest to ward off the chill of dusk. A breeze lifted the needles on the branches above her head. She should go back to the hotel for it was getting colder by the second. Yet she lingered, unwilling to relinquish the peace and utter stillness of her hideaway.

James stared at the crimson-clad figure perched on the boulder, wondering what she was doing there. He had just spent the better part of two hours walking around town looking for her, and here she was. He jammed his hands into his cocoa coat, his eyes focused on her still form and pure profile. Just for a moment a twinge of doubt assailed him about the plan, but he pushed it away. He didn't intend to seduce Isis; he was only going to romance her a little. In her business, she had to know the score. She wouldn't be hurt, he assured himself. After all, he wouldn't be taking advantage of her in any way. He grimaced at his mental arguments, acknowledging how much he disliked what he was about to do. If time weren't so damned short, he'd find another way.

Squaring his shoulders, he cleared his expression, knowing he had wasted enough of the hours left to him. He had to act. He walked toward her, preparing himself for the moment when she would turn and be aware of him.

Isis heard the crunch of footsteps on the path as she rose to leave. She lifted her eyes to the lone figure coming nearer. Recognition was slow. He was nearly upon her before she realized it was James.

"James," she breathed, surprised at the change in him. This was unassuming? Nice? Bland? Hah! Her gaze roamed over his deep chocolate jacket and the cream turtleneck caressing his chin. Dark brown jeans hugged his lean hips and legs to end in supple tooled-leather boots. Here was the visual evidence of the power she had sensed last night. She studied his face, dazed to see strength in the features she had thought so unremarkable. Even his hair had taken on a new personality, appearing rich with hidden highlights and a mind of its own as it fell in a thick wave across his forehead. The change was as startling as it was unnerving.

"Isis." He greeted her softly, finding it was no effort at all to convey his pleasure in seeing her again. For a moment he stared into her extraordinary eyes, seeing beyond the drama of her makeup to the woman beneath. Emotions swirled in the night-blue depths, drawing him closer. He blinked in an attempt to dispel the enchantment she unconsciously wove about him. He had to remember his plan.

"What are you doing down here?" Isis asked, hunching against the quickening breeze.

"Looking for you," he explained before gesturing back toward the way he had come. "May I walk you to the hotel?"

Isis inclined her head. "If you like." She fell into step beside him after giving him a puzzled glance. "Why did you want to find me?"

"I wanted to invite you to have dinner with me," he replied with a disarming smile.

"I don't know you," she pointed out gravely, stopping on the path to face him.

James looked blank. "What?" He stared at her, unable to believe she meant what she said.

"I had a drink with a man named James Leland last night, but he's not here now." She paused for a second, playing with the urge to divine his thoughts. She pushed it away. It wouldn't be fair. It was all right when he approached her the way he had last evening. Then her actions had been motivated by self-protection in an unexpected situation. But that was not the case now.

"What do you mean?" he demanded, playing his assigned role carefully. How much did she know? Had she lifted his intentions from his mind? Could she? He believed in ESP—what thinking person didn't? But how strong were her abilities? How accurate?

"Who are you, James Leland? What do you do?" she questioned in return. Her integrity might prohibit her from delving into his motives in her own special way, but it didn't preclude questions.

"Don't you know, goddess of the Nile? Mind reader *extraordinaire*?" he parried, doing a little probing himself.

Isis drew back, both physically and mentally, from the stinging edge she detected in his voice. "I do not invade any being's privacy unaware. I never have, I never will. My gift, if you can call it that, has certain responsibilities. I try to respect them so I can respect myself." She turned away, oddly disappointed in his attitude.

He had blown it, he chastised himself on seeing her expression. He couldn't let her leave. He had to soothe her ruffled feathers.

"Isis, wait," he commanded, catching her arm and swinging her around. The hastily erased pain on her face arrested the calculated words of apology he was about to deliver. "I'm sorry." The simple, sincere words escaped without thought. "I've hurt you, but I don't know how."

Isis shrugged uncomfortably. Why had she defended herself? She hadn't done that in years. "It's nothing." She shivered in a sudden gust of cold air. "I'm cold. Let's go back."

"Only if you tell me what I did," he agreed without releasing her.

Isis shifted, seeking to slide out of his hold. But his fingers tightened, binding her even closer to him. "We're both going to freeze," she warned him irritably.

He shook his head, his lips quirking in a lopsided half smile. "Nope, you're smarter than that. You'll give in now and promise retaliation later," he hazarded, watching her with an enigmatic gleam in his eyes.

Isis distrusted his expression almost as much as she distrusted his softening tone. The silky cadence was pleasing to her ear, but it grated on every other one of her senses. It demanded compliance by its sheer lack of force.

"All right," she capitulated, doing exactly as he predicted. Annoying man. "I spent most of my life discovering what an oddity I am. Before I was twenty, I'd been in places and done things most adults had never dreamed of. I've lived in palaces and tents, ridden Arabian stallions, camels and elephants. I've played in marketplaces with snake charmers and harem girls. I've lived in a world where a cup of water was worth more than a human life. I speak four languages fluently, read some ancient hieroglyphics and I read minds. The only place I've ever fit in, even marginally, is in this fake world of show business. Here I'm one oddity among a host of others.

"I know I'm unusual, but that doesn't mean I don't have values and ethics. All my life I've been judged by what others think is normal." She touched her brilliantly hued jacket, then her exotically painted face. "There are many who label me because of my clothes and my makeup." She stared at him with unflinching directness. "In a way, I think you're one of them. And that I don't want or need."

She sighed, suddenly tired of fighting a battle she would only lose again. "I don't know why you sought me out last night or today. But I do know it wasn't because of curiosity about my psychic power or interest in me as a person."

"You're wrong," he interrupted swiftly, needing to erase the disillusionment he glimpsed in her eyes. Damn her for being so sensitive. Why couldn't she have been tough and invulnerable? He didn't need this complication, but he couldn't walk away from her pain. Something stronger than the job he had to do demanded he comfort her.

"I do want to know you. I'll admit I've made some stupid assumptions, but that doesn't mean I can't change them or that I don't want to." He drew her toward him. "You have the kind of beauty a man could get lost in and count himself lucky in his fate. Yet there's gentleness in you, too, in spite of your gypsy-wild wardrobe and cosmetic artistry. You remind me of an anthurium bloom. You're so vibrantly alive with color, so perfectly formed you appear unreal. Yet the more I look, the closer I get, the more I want to learn about you."

He lifted his hand to her cheek, his gaze tracing her features to linger finally on her lips. "Let me start again without the impressions I erroneously formed. Show me who you are," he whispered deeply. Every plan, intention and approach was gone, leaving only the truth of the emotion she stirred in him.

"For only a day?" Isis countered, almost believing him. "I leave for home tomorrow. What good would twenty-four hours do either of us?"

"I don't have to spend my vacation here," he offered, wrapping his arm around her waist. He pressed his hand against the base of her spine, urging her closer. "I could get a room near your place, then we could see each other."

Isis searched his eyes, a little startled at the pleading urgency of his voice. Could he really want to be with her that much? Could she believe him? She wanted to but something held her back. "Surely you have plans?" she protested.

"Nothing I can't change," he denied quickly. He slipped his hand beneath the hair at her nape. "Invite me to follow you. I want to more than you can possibly know.'' He bent his head slightly to catch the ripe fullness of her lips, giving her a long second to evade his kiss.

Isis felt the light feather of his fingers, heard his breath sigh out when her eyes closed, accepting his caress. His kiss was a gentle warmth moving over her mouth, a sweet tide she welcomed. Instinctively, her lips softened in surrender and invitation all at once. He kissed her with a restraint and thoroughness that made her moan.

And then he changed, his arms closing around her, his caress deepening with a hunger as pervasive as the dusk converging into night. His masculine contours flowed against her until she fit him perfectly. With a small sound, she clung to him, melting in his heat and the velvet demands of his tongue. In that moment she responded to him as she had to no other man before him.

When he finally lifted his head, she was barely able to breathe. He stared into her eyes, inhaling deeply, his body against hers, very hard and very male. His voice was husky to the point of roughness when he spoke.

''Tell me you don't want to know me better. Tell me you don't need me to know you better. I won't believe you can walk away from this.''

''I can't,'' she confessed softly. She saw the flicker of satisfaction in his eyes and stiffened slightly in wariness. Her business carried an image of promiscuity and permissiveness many believed. ''But that doesn't mean I'm prepared to act on this.'' She waved her hand, graphically indicating their intimate position. ''I don't do indiscriminate relationships,'' she added just in case she had failed to make her point.

James's expression tautened with understanding. "I never thought you did," he denied, releasing her to step back a pace. "Believe it or not, that's not my style either."

For a long moment Isis stared at him, measuring his words against the information of her senses. She could probe his mind to gain the reassurance she needed, but she would not. Her well-honed instincts were enough of an edge in this age-old ritual of attraction.

"I believe you."

At her simple declaration he smiled, unwilling to admit even to himself how important her trust was. He held out a hand, palm up, a mute invitation for her touch.

Isis placed her fingers in his and found them swiftly enclosed in the warmth of his grasp.

"How long do we have before you need to get ready for the first show?" he asked as they started walking back the way they had come.

"A little over three hours. Why?" She glanced at him inquiringly.

"Have you forgotten my dinner offer already?" he responded, snagging her gaze with a quick demand. "I thought a lady of your perception would be above such an ordinary failing."

Isis grimaced at the mistaken belief held in his teasing remark. "So many people treat sensitives as though they are something of a freak or superhuman. Yet neither is true. We're simply people with special skills. Talents that nearly everyone on this earth has to some degree or could have if they chose to learn how to develop the power of their own brain."

Startled by her swift defense, James frowned. "Do you really believe that?" he questioned with obvious skepticism.

"Haven't you ever had a feeling that something specific was going to happen and it did? Had a hunch you acted on and had it pay off? Or been thinking about someone you hadn't seen or expected to visit and have them show up?"

"Of course I have, but that's only coincidence, not ESP," he returned firmly.

"Is it?" She stopped, turning to face him. She rarely climbed on her soapbox but this one time she felt an urgent need to make him see her and her power for what they were. "Why must paranormal ability be reserved for only a handful of beings, out of all mankind?"

James was silenced by her confounding question. Intellectually, he knew ESP existed. Innumerable studies and experiments had been conducted in many of the world's major learning centers to prove its validity. Yet now, faced with a living, breathing example of one of these gifted people, he found himself at a loss.

Isis sighed, easily reading the blankness in his eyes. "Forget I said anything. You can't help what you are any more than I can change what I am."

"Dont't lump me in with the rest of the uninformed," he shot back sharply. "Teach me."

"Why? What does this have to do with us?" She eyed him challengingly, although part of her was elated at the interest he showed in something he barely recognized.

"That's a stupid question. Your ability is an integral part of you. I can't get to know you better if I don't learn more about your power."

Isis shook her head, wanting to believe he was sincere, yet unable to shake the sudden memory of those seconds of telepathy they had shared the night before. "What about the sapphires, diamonds and Metcalf?" she demanded, acting on instinct. She studied his reaction to her abrupt question shrewdly.

The flicker of his lashes was scarcely perceptible, as was the faint tension invading his body. But she saw both responses, reading more than others would have in the telltale whispers of betrayal.

James forced himself to relax, knowing those mysterious dark eyes had already cataloged his involuntary starts. He should have been alert to just this possibility. "I thought you didn't peek into minds?" he parried dryly.

"I don't intentionally. But I also can't always control the input from a highly concentrated thought pattern." She waited, having no idea what to expect but knowing she could go no further until she had some answers.

James urged her down the path in a slow stroll. "I've been commissioned to find a certain necklace, which I believe Metcalf has. That's part of the reason I'm here. The rest is as I told you. I'm on a vacation," he explained casually. He tossed her a quick grin. "Nothing nefarious, I assure you." He met her gaze, secure in the knowledge she would see nothing more than what he told her in his mind or his expression. His training and experience had served him well, even when he was matched against one such as she.

"I've already had my dinner," Isis murmured, abruptly changing the subject. Satisfied with his explanation, she saw no point in further discussion.

James reached across in front of her to push open the hotel door. "Why so early?" he asked, taking his cue easily. "Surely you don't get nervous before you go on?"

"No, I—" She paused, her gaze resting on the desk clerk as he signaled her to him. "It looks like I'm being paged."

James nodded, already altering their route to stop at the main desk.

"Mrs. Sullivan is waiting for you upstairs, Ms O'Shea," the younger man said the moment Isis reached him. "She asked me to tell you she's having dinner sent up to your suite."

Isis frowned, her eyes darkening with annoyance as she turned away. "Sometimes—" she groaned, stifling a sharp expression with effort.

"Who's Mrs. Sullivan?" James queried, matching her quick stride through the crowded lobby to the elevators.

"My dresser and my friend, I think," she murmured absently, while wondering what had possessed Josie to order a meal from room service. The older woman knew she only ate once a day when she was on tour.

James studied her openly, surprised and a little puzzled by her reaction. "Would you mind explaining what exactly is wrong?"

Isis glanced at him, suddenly realizing he was still with her. "A small battle of wills," she replied with a slight dismissive shrug. "We'll have to postpone our evening until after my last show." The elevator opened and she stepped into the corridor. "You don't mind, do you?" She started down the hallway to her room.

"As a matter of fact, I do," James disagreed, catching her arm in a firm but gentle grip. "We had a date, remember?"

Isis halted in front of the door, then swung around to confront him. "I'll see you later, I promise."

James shook his head, his expression cast in determined lines. "Not good enough. A promise is a promise." He plucked the key she held from her hand to insert it smoothly in the lock.

Stunned at his actions as well as his attitude, Isis was slow in responding. He had the door open before she could even form a verbal protest. "You have no—" she began as he urged her inside.

"Right," he finished for her. "True, but I'd like to if you'd agree." A quick grin slashed his face, lighting his eyes with a challenging gleam. He opened his mouth to add something more, but never got the chance.

"It's about time you showed up. The food has arrived and it's getting cold." Josie marched across the sitting room, a glare darkening her features. "You stayed out way too long. You're probably frozen through and you should know better," she scolded, quickly slipping the jacket from Isis's shoulders. She turned, eyeing James balefully. "Were you with her?"

Bemused by the small woman's chastising manner and her take-charge approach, he found himself nodding automatically.

"Why didn't you get her indoors? Couldn't you tell how cold it was out there with the sun down? The wind off that lake is like an arctic blast."

"Josephine Sullivan, that's enough," Isis intervened hastily, knowing her friend was well into her role as self-appointed guardian.

Josie touched her cheek in a swift assessment. "Just as I thought, ice cold." She inclined her head in regal satisfaction, completely ignoring her employer's warning, if she even heard it. "I had the boy set the table near the fire. You can warm up and eat at the same time."

Isis's eyes flashed with rising temper. "I said—"

"—That's an excellent idea," James interrupted smoothly, taking her arm and shepherding her toward the sofa. "I'm starving."

Isis pulled away, trying to escape his hold without success. She gave him an annoyed look. "Let go of me," she hissed.

"Behave," he commanded tersely, "and I'll handle her for you."

Somehow Isis found herself ensconced comfortably on the couch, a small glass of sherry in her hand. Before her amazed eyes James became a charming, apologetic male, with Josie visibly relaxing under his expert handling. In a matter of minutes her friend was smiling and nodding her acceptance of his presence.

"See that she eats a good dinner," she ordered, giving Isis a knowing look. "Especially the Black Forest torte. It's her favorite dessert and she needs the calories."

"I'll do that," James agreed meekly, fixing Isis with a commanding stare that denied her the right to say a word.

Isis calmly sipped her drink, having no intention of trying to deal with Josie's mothering and James's strange possessiveness at the same time. She was content to let them make their little plans like two conspirators. All their neat schemes would only work if she chose to submit to them, and docility was far from being her most outstanding virtue, as she well knew. In fact, she could be amazingly stubborn given the right circumstances. As Josie was fully aware. And James was soon to be.

Three

Finally we're alone,'' James teased, a lopsided grin curving his mouth. He poured himself a sherry before joining Isis on the sofa.

"Pleased with yourself, are you?" she asked with seemingly idle interest. She shifted on the cushion, bending one knee at a comfortable angle.

He nodded, his hazel eyes alive with male satisfaction. "You'll have to admit my way was much easier than losing your temper," he pointed out calmly.

Isis lifted her glass to her lips and took a tiny sip while wondering if James was being deliberately obtuse. Didn't he realize how irritated his interference made her? "Contrary to your and Josie's beliefs, I do not need a keeper," she stated slowly, her unusually accented voice flowing with smooth precision over the clearly spaced words. She watched his head come up and his smile fade.

"I never thought you did," he parried neutrally, his gaze alert to her stillness. "As far as I could see it was my fault you were gone so long. I was simply doing what I could to make amends." He leaned forward to place his drink on the low table in front of him. He held out his hand, mutely offering to take the empty glass. "Doesn't anyone in your circle treat you with the gentleness you deserve?" One brow slanted upward, subtly altering his nice-guy features into a much more dynamic aura. "Every time I offer you even the smallest courtesy, you hesitate as you did now. Why?"

Isis stared at him, then at the crystal she held. Did she really do as he said? Thinking back, she had to agree, whether she realized it or not, she did. Slowly, oddly surprised at how difficult it was, she extended her goblet. His fingers closed around hers, drawing her eyes to his as he took the glass and placed it beside his. The changing hazel depths were filled with green shadows and flashes of golden brown. The warmth of their color radiated out, soothing her, gentling her independence for a moment.

"I've been on my own for fifteen years now. I'm used to running my life my way," she murmured quietly. "But even before that, I was always a loner."

"Out of choice, or because you're different?"

Isis's eyes widened briefly at his blunt question before her lashes dropped to shield her expression. "Does it matter?" she returned evasively.

James covered her fingers with his, cradling their slenderness in his palms without actually holding them. "I think it does, but I also think it's too soon to expect you to answer me." He frowned, wondering at the complexity of this exotic creature. She was nothing like the woman he had expected to find. "Come, let's eat," he suggested, using words to cloak the reminder of what he must have from her. He didn't want to remember why he had sought her out.

Isis rose, allowing her hands to remain in his, although she could easily have broken the tenuous contact. But for some reason, perhaps because of the illusion of freedom his light hold conveyed, she had no desire to deny herself the pleasure of his touch. And it was a pleasure, she acknowledged, as he seated her at the small table in the windowed alcove overlooking the lakeshore. The heat from the fireplace radiated out in gentle waves to dispel the lingering chill of her stroll.

"I'm really not hungry," she murmured, eyeing the attractively displayed dishes he uncovered with a minimum of fuss.

"I'll make a deal with you," James offered after taking his place across from her. "You put enough on your plate so that neither of us will be forced to lie to your guardian dragon, and I'll consume the lion's share of this meal."

Isis glanced at his serious face, then at the laden table. Josie appeared to have ordered every one of her favorite foods, from the fresh, steamed broccoli spears in butter sauce to the tempting trout almandine and the luscious Black Forest torte.

"Do you think you can?" She smiled, suddenly enjoying the prospect of seeing him outflanked by an overabundant menu.

James tipped his head, studying the dare sparkling in her eyes. "The only way you'll find out is by having a taste of everything here."

Sapphire eyes met hazel, each mirroring a depth of purpose far exceeding the importance of the small wager.

"You're on," Isis agreed, picking up her plate.

"Tell me about your act," he suggested, giving her a quick look while he served himself from the various platters.

"What do you want to know?"

He shrugged. "For one thing, do you actually read minds when you're out there, or are you doing some kind of mental sleight of hand?" He expertly uncorked the light white wine to pour them each a glass.

Isis cut into a perfectly prepared broccoli tuft and took a bite, savoring the crisp-textured vegetable in its delicate sauce. "A little of both," she admitted finally, pausing between nibbles. "Telepathy is a very inconsistent skill, or at least it is with me. I have to be in a receptive state and even then it's not always possible to tune in." She sipped her wine as she sought for the words to describe her performance. "I use a great deal of reading body language to work an audience. You'd be surprised at how much people give away with small movements of their lashes, an indrawn breath, flared nostrils, dilated eyes; even stillness or focused attention can betray one's thoughts. And those are just the little things nearly everyone misses. There are many more obvious signals."

"So you don't actually read thoughts, at least not usually."

She shook her head before absently adding another small piece of fish to her empty plate. "I read yours last night," she reminded him. "Actually, I did three, including yours." She waved her fork in a slow arc. "That's how I ended up in the casino. I was unwinding. When I have a really intense night, I usually have trouble sleeping although I'm exhausted."

"Hence the redoubtable Josie's clucking," he deduced with a crooked smile.

She nodded, acknowledging the accuracy of his guesswork. "She's a little aggravated with me because of the length of this tour. She thinks it's too much of a physical drain."

James glanced up at her sharply, for the first time noticing the faint shadows visible beneath her makeup. "And is it?" he demanded abruptly, surprised at the concern he felt for her well-being.

"Possibly," she admitted after an obvious hesitation.

"Why did you agree? Surely you knew what a schedule like this would mean? You've certainly been in the business long enough," he commented, watching her closely. He knew he was being far too personal but he was incapable of stifling his questions.

"If I didn't know better, I'd swear you were kin to Josie," she teased in an effort to lighten the atmosphere. Fleetingly, she wondered why she was even allowing his familiarity. His attitude was far beyond a twice-met acquaintance. In fact, it was closer to proprietary, she decided on seeing the grim look in his eyes at her banter.

"If you want to tell me to back off, do it," he commanded tersely. "But don't hide behind some polite evasion when you think I've overstepped the mark. Those tactics aren't necessary with me, either now or in the future."

Taken back at the swift display of temper, Isis fingered her wineglass in silence. Her lashes fanned her cheeks in a self-defensive screen. He had gone beyond the limits she usually set, yet she was curiously reluctant to reprimand him. And that bothered her far more than any action on his part.

"It's getting late," she murmured, glancing at him. It was an evasion. She knew it and she saw by his expression he did, too.

"I'll leave right after dessert," he promised, his eyes alight with a no-nonsense gleam she was beginning to recognize. "Don't forget you gave me your word." He watched a flicker of rebellion flare to life in the extraordinary depths of her eyes, then die as she shrugged her mute acquiescence.

He reached for a small plate beside the cake stand. He was pushing her. He recognized the fact even as he ignored it. Something about this woman touched a protective chord within him. The need to care for her was as unexpected as it was powerful. It wasn't that he doubted her strength or ability to care for herself. It was simply that he had the strangest feeling she never noticed her physical requirements. Perhaps it was her other-worldly presence, the fragile, breakable quality of her slender body, or possibly even the foreign mystique surrounding her. She was unlike any female he had ever known. She intrigued him, baffled him and enticed him beyond the very real reason he had pursued her.

Isis stared down at the thin sliver of rich dessert before her. Much as she enjoyed the dark chocolate treat, she was in no mood to savor it at this moment. Her reaction to James and his to her were confusing and not a little bewildering. At thirty-two, she should be well past the unpredictabilities of sheer sexual attraction, if she ever had been susceptible. Yet there was no denying her own body's traitorous signals or the cracks in her barriers of self-sufficiency. She ate the last bit of cake slowly, privately amazed at how ambivalent her feelings were. Push him away or allow him to stay?

She placed her fork carefully on the empty plate and lifted her eyes to his. "If I asked you to let me try to read your mind, would you allow it?" she questioned, prompted by an impulse she barely understood.

He smiled slowly, his mouth quirking at the polite formality of her request. "No, you have too much of an edge as it is. A man must have a few secrets." How exquisite she was in her rainbow-vivid clothes and silver-gilded makeup. Anyone else would have appeared as a theatrical doll, but not Isis. Her usual image somehow fit the rare creation she was.

"What edge?" Isis asked, genuinely perplexed.

James's eyes softened at the uncertainty of her reply. He was sure she recognized her physical beauty simply by the way she dressed to enhance it. Yet she chose to ignore it just as she underplayed her paranormal talents. She was amazingly untouched by conceit, yet at the same time no one could doubt the surety she felt of her own self-worth. It was in that belief that her strength lay.

"I'm not telling," he parried, rising to his feet. He was well aware that it was getting close to show time. Josie had warned him to allow her at least two hours to prepare.

Isis got up, knowing he was leaving as promised. She subdued the flicker of disappointment she felt at his easy compliance. "You're not playing fair," she accused softly, following him to the door.

James paused, his back to her as the husky protest sliced through him. If she knew— He clamped his teeth shut against the secret he guarded. It took every ounce of will he had to blank from his expression the distaste he felt for this secrecy. He consoled himself with the knowledge that he would allow his interests to be satisfied only so far. He wouldn't take advantage of her for the sake of his own self-respect and his respect for her.

"I always play fair," he stated deeply, swinging around to confront her. "If you believe anything about me, believe that." He slipped his hands over her shoulders, staring intently into her luminous blue velvet eyes. "Promise you'll remember."

Isis searched his features, easily seeing the strength hidden beneath the ordinary composition of lines and planes. "I promise," she agreed on a sigh, wondering at the intensity of his demand, yet unable to deny him his request.

His eyes glowed with shades of colors and emotion at her soft agreement. He smiled as the tension flowed out of him. James lowered his lips to hers, barely touching them, using the tip of his tongue to circle the lush outline with a tantalizing caress. She stood still beneath his touch, encouraging him to trace the moist inducement along her cheek to the hollow of her throat. His breath was a warm whisper when he explored the sensitive spot behind her ear.

Isis quivered as shivers of pleasurable delight washed over her at his delicately erotic lovemaking. The restraint he showed, the lack of the usual embrace were as beguiling as the gentleness of his seduction. He made no attempt to stroke or hold her nearer when she arched invitingly against him.

At the first sign of her active participation, James pulled away. Her quickened breathing pleased him even as he berated himself for arousing her when he knew he would not satisfy her. A male tease, he castigated himself in disgust. "I'll be in the audience tonight," he told her, self-directed anger making his voice rougher than he intended. The flicker of surprised bewilderment in her eyes as he turned quickly away only added to his guilt. Damn her for being as vulnerable as she was.

Isis stared after his rigid, retreating back, wondering what had happened. One moment they had been so close and the next she had sensed waves of hostility searing her skin. She shook her head over the contradictory phenomenon. She crossed the room to stand staring at the table. The empty serving dishes were a mute testimony to the meal they had shared.

Empty? Suddenly the significance of the clean plates sank in. A slow smile curved her lips as she realized James had outmaneuvered her and she had never noticed. She had been so busy fielding his questions, she had eaten another dinner and enjoyed it. Josie certainly had a conspirator in James.

She cast a glance at her watch, realizing time was slipping away. She still had meditation to do before she went downstairs to the dressing room. "The last night," she murmured as she disconnected the phone from its jack, then switched off the lights and put out the Do Not Disturb sign.

She settled into a comfortable position on the sofa, her eyes focused on the twinkling stars visible through the night-shrouded windows. James's image intruded on the peaceful heavenly canvas, inhibiting her slow relaxation breathing with quicksilver flashes of memory. For a moment Isis allowed his presence to linger in her mind, savoring the warm excitement flowing through her to destroy her concentration. Then, knowing she must, she gently banished the vision, emptying her mind of all thought.

She inhaled deeply, evenly, listening to the sound of the measured cadence. In. Out. She floated free, lifting up and out in a mental stretch. She hovered on the unseen plane, superaware and yet beyond awareness, too. She was in a familiar, relaxing, stress-free place that few knew but all could experience if they chose. Time had no meaning in this altered state of consciousness.

She came back to reality slowly, feeling the gentle euphoria she privately called bliss surrounding her. She rose and walked through to the bathroom, shedding clothes as she passed. She stepped into a warm shower, delighting in the rush of heated water over her body.

James. His name whispered across the silence, melting into her receptive thoughts like gentle rain. He was and he wasn't as he seemed to be. Secrets lurked behind his sometimes unassuming exterior. Yet truth also waited in the shadows in the guise of the attraction he felt for her. Her experience, while not as vast as her entertainment-world inhabitation might suggest, was great enough to reinforce her belief. But even now when her senses were crystal clear of outside pressure, she still felt something was not as it should be.

She stepped out of the shower, dried and donned another caftan. This time it was one fashioned of the fiery colors of a desert sunset, designed to swirl about her supple body in clouds of dragonfly-wings gauze. She brushed her hair, allowing the dull ebony fall to lie straight against her back to her waist. She avoided the mirror during her preparation, knowing from experience how plain her unmade-up face appeared without its usual meticulously applied cosmetics. She slid her feet into a soft pair of Moroccan slippers adorned with silver tassels and tiny bells before gliding out of her suite for the short ride downstairs to her dressing room.

"If I had known James was going to take care of you this well, I wouldn't have worried one bit," Josie remarked, eyeing Isis with undisguised satisfaction the moment she entered. "There's some color in your cheeks for a change and a definite improvement in those shadows."

Isis grimaced, giving her friend a warning look. "If I didn't depend on you so much," she shot back pointedly, a faint sting in her tone.

Josie nodded, undisturbed by the half-finished promise of retribution. "You'd fire me, I know." She chuckled smugly as she prodded her charge into a chair. "Do it tomorrow," she advised, deftly beginning the elaborate stage preparations she excelled in. "Right now, we've got to get you ready."

Isis gazed at her in the mirror, her expression rueful. "I should never have let myself be conned into letting you traipse around the country with me. I'll bet Ned's blessing the day I took you off his hands."

Josie laughed, her eyes twinkling at Isis's words. "Don't you malign my husband," she responded pertly. "I'll have you know I'm following *his* orders to keep an eye on you. You'd forget to feed yourself if I weren't around to keep you on track."

Isis suppressed the telltale quiver of her lips, determined to hold on to her hard-won annoyance. "You cheated this time bringing in an outsider," she reminded her accusingly.

Josie shrugged, not in the least put out by her charge. "Worked, didn't it?" With practiced ease she twisted the long black plait she had just finished into a high chignon. "Besides, I think James's present status is temporary at best."

Isis's delicate brow rose at the certainty in her voice. "Oh?"

Josie turned Isis's chair to begin her makeup. "I saw the way he acted. You can't tell me that man's not interested." She applied foundation carefully. "Even if he doesn't look like anything special, he's still got something about him." She paused, obviously searching for a description. "Aura—that's it." She stared at Isis. "You felt it, too. I could tell."

Isis debated denying Josie's observations, but decided against it. It was useless to pretend she didn't know what Josie meant. Josie was amazingly perceptive when she chose to be. "I noticed," she agreed dryly. "What I can't figure out is why me?"

"Are you blind, woman? Why not you?" Josie demanded, her eyes flashing indignantly.

Isis shook her head, unable to explain away the vague uneasiness she felt. "Why not indeed?" she murmured appeasingly.

Four

—

The applause thundered in the main room as the audience loudly proclaimed its awe of Isis's ability. James clapped appreciatively along with the rest of the people around him while he stared at Isis in her place at center stage. She really was an extraordinary entertainer. No one seemed to care whether her act was the result of expert guesses or true psychic talent. They were too enthralled with her dazzling costumes, her mysterious, alluring image and the unreal atmosphere she spun so effortlessly.

James watched the curtain drift shut, as unwilling as the rest of them to let go of the sorcery she had displayed. The calls of "More!" "Encore!" and "Isis!" echoed his own thoughts with uncanny precision, and he was amazed at himself. He had sat through three other nights just like this one, never actually seeing or being affected by Isis and her unique artistry. He had been too involved with keeping an eye on Burt Metcalf and figuring an innocent way to get into his estate. But this evening he had taken only enough time to notice the owner was in his usual place before he had turned his attention to the stage. From that moment on, he had lost all interest in anyone or anything else.

Rising to his feet, he signaled the waitress for his bill. Automatically he glanced toward the reserved table Metcalf occupied tonight. His seat was empty. James stiffened alertly, his eyes scanning the crowd to catch a glimpse of Metcalf's stocky frame. A flash of formal black disappearing through the side door leading backstage drew his gaze.

Every sense flared to life. Was this the chance he'd been waiting for? Was his man making Isis another offer? Hopefully, one she would not refuse this time. Deftly winding his way between tables, he headed for the door through which Metcalf had passed. He got no farther than the gray-suited man standing guard just inside.

"I'm sorry, sir, but this area's off limits to the patrons," he informed him politely.

James hesitated, feeling fairly certain if he gave Isis's name, he would gain admittance once she was informed of his presence. But he hated using her yet again. Frowning at the tug of his conscience, he glanced past the burly shoulder partially obscuring his vision. The sight of Josie's thin figure was as unexpected as it was welcome.

"Josie," he called, lifting his voice slightly above the noise around him.

Josie jerked to a stop, glancing around in surprise. "James, what are you doing here?" she questioned, moving quickly toward him. "Was Isis expecting you?

She didn't mention it." She gave his muscled watchdog a strained smile. "It's all right, Sam. I know him." She caught James's arm, urging him along the long corridor leading away from the stage area. "Come on, I'll show you where we are."

"Wait a minute," he commanded, bringing Josie to a confused halt. "What's wrong?"

She shook her head, glancing at him briefly before looking away again. "Don't you want to see Isis?" she questioned in turn.

"Yes," he replied impatiently, eyeing her unconcealed agitation assessingly. "Trust me, Josie. Something has upset you. Let me help." He waited, mentally grinding his teeth at the older woman's silence. "Is it Isis? Is she ill?" He tried again, voicing the only two possibilities he could think of that would produce such an extreme reaction.

"No, she's not sick, but if that man doesn't quit nagging at her, she might end up that way," she snapped angrily, her features reflecting her anxious concern.

"What man?" James asked, having a very good idea whom she would name.

"Burt Metcalf. His wife's very interested in Isis's psychic abilities because she thinks she may be paranormal, too. She wants to have Isis at a party they're giving," she explained briefly, impatiently. She gazed down the hall, then back to his face. "You can get rid of him. You know how tired she was. I told him to at least wait until she got out of her costume before he talked to her, but he wouldn't listen," she muttered half to herself. "He just won't accept that Isis doesn't do private gigs anymore." Josie pinned him with a pleading look. "Couldn't you get rid of him? Tell him you two have a date or something. I know it's an imposition, what with you barely knowing us and all. But please try."

James hesitated, caught between the needs that had brought him halfway across the country and the worry he felt for the intriguing woman he had just begun to know.

"Please," she entreated. "Isis won't do it herself. She never turns anyone away."

"All right," he agreed finally, giving in to his protective instinct. "I'll rescue your ewe lamb." He touched Josie's arm lightly in reassurance. "Lead the way."

Giving him a grateful smile, she quickly guided him to Isis's dressing room. The sound of a masculine voice tinged with frustration was clearly audible through the closed door.

James gestured Josie aside as he turned the handle to enter. "Not ready yet, honey?" he observed casually as he strolled toward Isis's motionless figure. He slipped an arm around her waist and pulled her against his side before focusing his attention on the man he had come to see. "I don't believe we've met."

Isis heard his words in a haze of weariness mixed with vague surprise at his appearance and possessive attitude. The introduction taking place between the two men rumbled unintelligibly in her ears as she relaxed against James's deceptively solid strength. She was so tired all she wanted was to sleep. Instead she had been forced to endure Burt Metcalf's increasingly persuasive demands to visit his estate. None of her arguments against her acceptance had had the slightest effect on the determined man. She had been nearing the end of her frazzled patience when James had materialized on her doorstep. Even the sight of Josie's familiar form hovering in the background hadn't brought the relief that seeing James had. She sighed, unconsciously snuggling closer.

James's arm tightened around Isis's scantily clad body. "Why don't you let Josie help you change while we step outside?" he suggested, giving Josie a commanding look. Josie hurried forward obediently, more than willing to comply.

Isis glanced at him, her eyes warm with gratitude. "You're coming back?" she questioned, knowing full well they had made no plans for the evening.

He brushed her lips with a quick kiss. "Ten minutes," he murmured softly before releasing her.

Isis nodded, then offered her visitor a brief goodbye. The moment the door closed leaving her and Josie blessedly alone, she sank down on the chair in front of the mirror. "Thanks for getting me out of that."

Josie plucked the pins from Isis's hair and began unbraiding it. "I didn't really. James was already on his way to see you. I just got him past the stage guard." She gazed at Isis in the mirror. "Why didn't you tell me you had a date?"

"Because I didn't," she replied simply. "I knew he was in the audience, but I hadn't expected to meet him after the show." She bent her head back, enjoying the soothing stroke of the brush through her long mane.

"I like him," Josie murmured after a short silence. "There's something about him that kind of gets to you. I don't think that what you see is what you get with that one."

Isis's lips curved at the decidedly impressed addition. She lifted her face to allow Josie to remove her makeup. "I noticed you and he got very friendly in an indecently short time," she observed, knowing she was inviting the sting of Josie's tongue.

The older woman shrugged, ignoring her mistress's teasing. "He's got a nice way about him. Not like some of these hot bod types we meet in this crazy business," she agreed with her usual blunt candor. "He knows how to make a woman feel special."

Isis rose, towering over her friend by several inches. "All of this on the basis of two meetings. I'm amazed at your perception."

Josie whisked her out of her rainbow gown and into a stark, white silk burnoose embroidered with orchids and birds of paradise. "You must like him, too," she pointed out swiftly. "In all the years I've been on the road with you, I've never known you to pair up with anyone before."

"Pair up?" Isis repeated, one delicate brow winging upward at her description. "I think that implies considerably more than there is."

Josie cast her a searching glance. "I wonder why you felt the need to explain that?"

"Josie, I—" Isis began only to swallow the rest of her warning when there was a knock at the door.

"Shall I let him in?" Josie questioned.

Isis stared at the closed panel, then at her reflection. "Tell him to wait a minute. I have to put my face on."

The older woman shook her head. "He's not going to care about that. Besides, I think you look much nicer without your paint."

Isis grimaced, seeing nothing attractive about her unadorned skin. After her elaborate stage artifice, she felt too plain for words. Only her dark eyes held any color and even they lacked their usual brilliance.

"Isis?" The worry in the masculine voice from the corridor held a note of command.

"Do something," she directed with a hurried glance at the unlocked door.

Josie moved to block the entrance a split second too late as James entered. "Why didn't you answer me?" he demanded, striding toward her, completely ignoring Josie's flimsy attempt to stop him.

Isis swung around to reach for the bottle of foundation on the table. "I haven't finished changing," she explained as calmly as she was able. She didn't need this now. Why hadn't he waited outside a little longer? At least until she was prepared to appear in public.

James halted abruptly, suddenly sensing something was wrong. He stared at Isis's rigid back, wondering what he had missed. "You don't need to go to the trouble of putting on makeup just for me. I realize you're wiped out." He reached out to still her cream-dotted fingers before they touched her skin.

Isis faced forward, giving him her profile. "Please, wait outside," she murmured, wishing she dared snatch her hand away. The warmth of his grip was like a silken shackle around her wrist and she chafed at the small imaginary bond.

James studied her set features, seeing no answer for her behavior revealed in the finely sculpted bone structure. He glanced over his shoulder at Josie. "Obviously I'm obtuse. She won't explain. Will you?"

"No, she won't," Isis snapped, giving her friend a warning glare.

Josie ignored both her words and irritation. "Isis has this thing about cosmetics. She flatly refuses to let anyone see her without her face, as she calls it."

"You're kidding," James muttered, releasing her hand. She was that vain? She couldn't be, he responded silently the second the thought was born. He gazed at her, noting the tension simmering beneath the vibrant gown. "Why, Isis?" he asked quietly as he took a seat on the chair beside the table.

She lifted her eyes to his, defiance glimmering in the lake-blue depths. "Why do you think?"

"It's not vanity," he stated, suddenly never more sure of anything than he was of that. "You can't be so blind you don't realize your own natural beauty."

"You don't know me so you can't be sure of what I think or feel," she replied, feeling goaded by his persistence. Why didn't he leave as she asked? He had no right to probe her mind.

"A mask." He gestured toward the extensive array of feminine artistry. "But why? You, of all people, should be beyond that sort of camouflage."

Isis forgot the presence of Josie, her exhaustion and the late hour. James had revealed her innermost fragile needs. He had brought to light something she had always kept secret. "You have no right to poke and prod into my personality," she retaliated huskily. "No being has the right unless it is freely offered to him."

James drew back as though she had struck him. Fool, he berated himself, knowing what she said was true. He had trespassed far beyond what their short acquaintance allowed. "How do I apologize?" he asked, watching her intently. "I was thoughtless as well as presumptuous. Will you forgive me?"

Annoyed though she was, she still heard the deep-felt sincerity of his words, finding a reflection of his remorse in his expression. For a long second, she held on to her irritation, then, unable to resist the masculine plea in his eyes, she nodded.

"Thank you," he murmured, lifting his fingers to gently stroke the velvety curve of her cheek. From the corner of his eye, he caught the flicker of movement as Josie left the room, soundlessly closing the door behind her. "I'll wait for you in the corridor." He stared at her, imprinting the purity of her ungilded features in his mind, a little shocked at the delicacy he found. Slowly, reluctantly he drew his fingers away from the warmth of her flesh.

"No, stay," Isis breathed, reacting to an internal demand that had no relation to her feelings or her past refusals to allow anyone so close to her inner self.

James halted midway between sitting and standing to search her face. "You're sure?"

She inclined her head, her eyes so dark they were but a step away from midnight. For a moment she lost herself in the emotions touching his expression. Relief, concern and pleasure were clear. But was that tenderness she saw swirling in the hazel fog of his eyes? She closed her lashes, dismissing the validity of her conclusions. Physically and mentally she was far more depleted than she had ever been in her life. Normally she trusted her "gift" implicitly, but not at this moment.

She opened her eyes and reached for her foundation once more, all the while conscious of James's unblinking attention. "I never wore this stuff until I came to the States," she explained absently as she began transforming her face into an Eastern dream of mystery. "When I was in Egypt it never mattered."

"And it does here?" James inserted, more to encourage the warm, honey flow of her voice with its strange hint of a foreign accent than to probe the delicate issue of her camouflage. Oddly, he had lost all interest in digging where he would cause her pain.

"It matters," she agreed, stroking a bronze cream blusher into her skin. "I thought coming back to the land of my birth would be a sort of homecoming, but it wasn't." She sighed, remembering the displaced feelings she had then and still had now more often than she liked. "This world is too civilized to accept the unusual without first dissecting the new specimen." She shook her head, disgusted at the way her thoughts were turning themselves into words. She hardly knew this man, yet she was practically baring her soul to him.

"You've really been raked over the coals because of your ability, haven't you?" James deduced, accurately reading the fleeting hurt in her eyes. "People are never kind to those they're jealous of."

Startled at his pronouncement, Isis swung toward him, her lips slightly parted in preparation for the final coat of lip color. "Jealous?" she repeated, as though she had never heard the word before. She frowned, turning the assessment over in her mind when he made no immediate answer. "That's crazy." She waved her hand impatiently, barely missing decorating his jaw with her lipstick. "One or two people, maybe, but a whole group? I've been branded a charlatan, a witch, a liar and a fake, and you call it jealousy."

He nodded, manfully suppressing a grin at her indignation. He dodged hastily as she gestured irritably once more. "Don't you think the rest of us mortals would give our last dollar to peek into another's mind, look back in time to locate something lost or maybe peer into the future before it arrives?" he demanded, amazed to discover the truth he felt in his own words.

"It doesn't work that way," she protested judiciously. "I'm not a futuristic video machine. Flip a switch and select a setting and out pops a prediction." She capped her lipstick and tossed it on the vanity in disgust. "Of all the idiotic—" she began, only to be interrupted by a muffled choke of laughter.

James tried and failed to hold back his amusement. At first he had only meant to ease the past's hold on her, but somewhere along the line his intentions had short-circuited. He had needed to wipe away the disillusioned weariness in her voice and in her eyes.

"What are you laughing about?" she demanded, glaring at him.

James looked her over, his eyes dancing with mischief. "Video machine? Really, Isis, couldn't you have picked a more believable comparison?" He tipped his head to study her delectably rounded form beneath its artfully decorated white covering.

Isis followed his glance, momentarily at a loss. It took a second for his audacious comment to penetrate her exhaustion-slowed mind. Her lips twitched as she finally made the connection. "It was a rather ill-advised observation," she agreed after giving the matter the consideration it deserved. She lifted her eyes to his. "How about a human-form robot?"

He shook his head, his expression suspiciously solemn. "Not unless the inventor had a magazine centerfold in mind." He folded his hands in his lap, somehow contriving to appear totally detached from the suggestive conversation. "In fact, he'd have to be something of a girl-of-the-month aficionado."

Isis bit her lip to contain the laughter threatening to bubble up in her throat. In spite of all the strange things she had done in her life, this conversation was a first.

Here she was, so tired she could barely hold her head up, discussing her physical attributes without the least hint of modesty or reserve with a man she had known only a little over twenty-four hours. The mind boggled at what they would talk about when a week was up.

"No comeback?" he teased, giving her a slight wink.

Whatever restraint she had died with his gesture. Isis's giggle grew into chuckles, then into outright hilarity, complete with tears enough to brim over in silver trails down her cheeks. "Blast you, James Leland," she gasped, rising unsteadily to her feet.

He caught her waist between his hands, supporting her despite his seated position. He stared up at her, his amusement giving way to a need to hold her close. "You have a beautiful laugh, Isis O'Shea. It fits you—fresh, joyous, yet with a husky throb a man could listen to deep in the center of the night."

Isis froze, suspended between the outpouring of her emotions and the warm cloak of feeling he held so invitingly open. One tiny move and the elusive, imaginary fabric would surround her. She would be in his arms.

James drew her slowly toward him until she stood with her legs against his right thigh. "Let me hold you." His words were a command and a plea. When she made no move to deny him, he pulled her gently down onto his lap.

Isis was barely aware of his actions. Her whole attention was centered on his face. Did he know his eyes smiled before his lips ever quirked into that lopsided grin so peculiarly his own? She lifted her hand to his jaw, lightly fingering the sharp angle of the long line. How alive he felt. Energy seemed to flow into her fingertips through the faintly rough rasp of his evening beard.

"Isis." Her name on his lips drew her gaze. Her fingers slipped over his square chin to the full curve of his lower lip. "Witch." Never had that word been uttered with so much feeling.

"James," she whispered, caught in the web they had magically spun together.

James drew her against his chest, arms tightening around her supple form with unconscious possession. "Give me your mouth, woman," he groaned, impelled by the deep force of basic man to claim his own.

Isis stared into the green-gold depths of his eyes, then his brown lashes swept down. He took her lips with a devastating blend of hunger and gentleness. His hand slipped beneath the hair at her nape, entangling in the heavy strands. The tip of his tongue traced her mouth, tantalizing until she obeyed his unspoken plea and opened her lips for his invasion.

He buried his fingers in her hair, his hold a gentle chain so that she was unable to offer anything less than he asked. Half in protest, half in response, she put her hands on his upper arms. The hidden strength in the flesh beneath her fingertips told her much about the hunger, the power and the restraint of this man called James. He could easily have forced the response he so obviously wanted from her.

But he hadn't. Instead, he held her as though she were a fragile treasure of infinite value. His body was a protective, heated cradle, his embrace a secure haven. He coaxed, rather than demanded, she accept the pleasure he found in her nearness. Never had she known such a feeling of absolute strength and safety.

When the velvet roughness of his tongue moved against hers, her hands slipped up his shoulders to his neck. Tentatively, then with greater assurance, she responded, touching the smoothness of his mouth, the slightly sharp edges of his teeth, the sweet taste of his breath, all the beguiling textures of him. When he shifted, one hand roaming slowly, seductively down her spine, she arched against his body for a long moment.

Then, with tangible reluctance, James lifted his head to gaze into her cloudy eyes. "Help me, Isis. I'm too hungry for you to walk away unless you give me the strength to do it."

"Why did you have to remember that right at this second?" she breathed deeply. The husky richness of her plea was evidence of her arousal.

"I want you too much for you to regret anything we share." His eyes traced the passion-softened line of her lips. "It's better now than later."

Isis closed her eyes and trembled as an unusual weakness invaded her at the promise his words seemed to hold. She looked up at him with dazed sapphire eyes, suddenly unsure of herself, afraid of him. "James..."

He kissed her gently, soothing her. "Come, I'll walk you back to your room," he offered, smiling at her crookedly. He rose with her in his arms. "Will you be able to sleep?"

"Yes," she murmured softly, her lips curving at the caring in his question.

He released her slowly, easing her down the length of his body until she stood facing him. "Will you call me when you get up?"

She nodded. "I still have to give you directions to my place."

He touched his forefinger to her lips to silence her. "Tomorrow when you're rested. There'll be plenty of time then." He tucked her hand in his. "Right now you need your bed and I need a walk by the lake."

Giving in to his reasonable arguments, Isis followed him to the door. "It's too cold out there now," she protested.

James gave her a significant look. "Believe me, honey, that's the general idea," he whispered against her ear as he leaned forward to open the door. "You're a potent mixture and I need to sober up."

Five

—

I don't suppose you'd care to tell me how I ended up in *my* car with *you* driving *me* home?" Isis questioned, staring at James's relaxed frame with a jaundiced eye.

He glanced at his decidedly colorful, if somewhat irritable passenger. "Got up on the wrong side of the bed this morning, did we?" he countered easily. "And here I thought you'd thank me for offering to transport you and your sleek little Trans-Am home."

"I'm perfectly capable of managing that feat myself." Isis stretched her legs to shift more comfortably into the bucket seat. "I like to drive. It relaxes me. Besides, now Ned will have to come down to pick up Josie at the hotel." She frowned, considering her dresser's sudden preoccupation with getting her costumes cleaned before she packed to head home. "Why do I get the feeling you and Josie are conspiring?" She studied him as she voiced her suspicion. In spite of her skill, Isis was unable to detect the slightest hint of a reaction to her demand.

James shrugged, his gaze never faltering from the winding road that ran along the lake's rugged northeast shore. "She's concerned about you. I ran into her in the lobby after I left you last night. When I mentioned I needed to rent a car to head up your way, she suggested this arrangement instead."

Isis groaned, well able to believe her mothering friend was capable of such well-meaning meddling. "You could have made up some excuse," she pointed out.

"I could have," he agreed, slanting her a quick, searing look. "But I didn't want to. I liked the idea of spending this time with you, and I'm just old-fashioned enough to enjoy being able to take care of you."

"Take care of—" Isis gasped, annoyed.

James ignored her muted outrage, interrupting her without compunction. "I know it's only a temporary state of affairs but I like it." He nodded once, his expression grave. "Occasionally a man needs to feel his woman depends on him. Boosts his ego, you know. Makes him want to leap tall buildings, race speeding bullets, lift railroad cars." A choke of smothered laughter punctuated his final example. He turned his head to see Isis vainly trying to remain angry. "Did you say something?"

She shook her head, knowing if she took her fingers away from her mouth to speak, she'd lose control.

"Are you sure?" he taunted with a straight face that was ruined by the deviltry lurking in his eyes.

"Just drive," Isis commanded, finally subduing her humor enough to say something. Momentarily she wondered what the penalty was for assaulting one's chauffeur. Darn him. He could charm a cobra into a teacup with that smile of his and the logical way he arranged things to suit himself. How could a normal person expect to cope with his brand of reason? "Don't you think you're taking over just a little too fast?"

"I don't have much time. Unlike you, I'm not a resident of this part of the country." He negotiated a sharp bend with consummate ease. "I'm only here on vacation."

"And to see Metcalf," Isis added without conscious thought, absently noting the subtle attractiveness of his face. The sunshine and shade through which they drove alternately camouflaged, then revealed his expression and his underlying strength. The play of light and dark was so reminiscent of his changing personality Isis shivered. James was an enigma. One moment self-effacing, the next second a strong hero-type. Both roles fit him so well it was difficult to decide who or what he was.

James paused for a brief second, thrown off balance to realize he had forgotten his main goal in being in Nevada. He'd never felt less like remembering his job. "There's that," he agreed, aware she had unknowingly offered the opening he needed. "I haven't had much luck in that department."

Isis detected a subtle change in his tone. Alert and curious without knowing why, she studied him carefully. "Why not? You could have approached him any time in the past four days."

"Don't you think I tried?" James gave her a quick, probing look.

Her thoughtful expression and the sympathetic softness in her eyes was exactly the reaction he wanted. He hated himself for this manipulation. Nora Harris was a long-valued friend with only a few measured sunrises left, but was she and the reconciliation of a third-generation feud worth this? It was the only way, he reminded himself, glancing back at the road to avoid seeing the generosity of the woman beside him.

"Maybe I could help," Isis suggested slowly. "Burt Metcalf is a fan and sometimes that can open closed doors."

James's hands tightened on the steering wheel. "Before last night that may have been true but not now. He wasn't pleased when you refused his request."

Isis's eyes narrowed in recollection. "Your stepping in didn't help your cause at all," she murmured, thinking aloud. He had done her a favor when he had fended off the other man. She would have liked to return the compliment. "It's too bad I don't do private shows anymore. I could have taken you along."

"Just what do you have against that kind of performance? A man like Metcalf would certainly make it worth your while."

"Moneywise I'd probably do very well with his gig, but most of the time that kind of appearance is a status-symbol thing, with me doing my tricks like a trained seal," she stated dryly, eyes darkening with memories of earlier jobs.

James eased the car off the road onto a wide, flat area lightly covered with snow. He switched off the engine, then turned in his seat to face her.

"Why are we stopping?" Isis stared first at him, then around the small clearing rimmed with evergreens.

He ignored her question to ask one of his own. "You don't really like being on show, do you?" he responded, knowing he was once again probing where he had no right.

Isis hesitated, torn between honesty and her normal reserve. Even Josie, who was closer to her than anyone, didn't realize how little she cared for public life.

"Don't shut me out. I really want to understand."

The deep, compellingly slow voice was rich with gentleness and sincerity, beckoning to her to trust him. It was a primitive call on the most basic of levels, a summons she was unable to refuse. "No," she admitted finally.

"Then why do it?"

"To eat, just like the rest of the world," she replied with a touch of sarcasm. "A man who makes music sells his talent to live, a housewife offers her abilities in compensation for her support. I read minds for a price."

"Don't," James commanded, catching her hands when she would have turned away. "Don't pretend to be a hard-boiled entertainer. You're not."

Isis shook her head, unknowingly tightening her fingers on his. "I should be. I've been in this business eight long years. It's hard to have any illusions after that." She lowered her lashes, her gaze focusing on their entwined hands. "Do I look like a librarian to you?"

The seeming irrelevance of her question startled James into a short crack of amused laughter. "No."

"Well, I am," she murmured, raising her eyes to catch his disbelieving expression. "I've got a master's in library science. A degree I used for a total of three months until the city arbitrators of policy politely suggested I either develop a more conventional bearing or I look for another line of work."

James stared at her, unable to imagine her unusual beauty and ability in the sedate setting of books, whispered conversation and supreme order. Isis was too much a creature of the elements. A spirit born to be free, to ride the winds of her extraordinary mind. But did she belong in the glitzy showcase she had chosen? Every instinct he possessed said she did not. And his instincts were seldom wrong. In his business he could ill afford to make an error in judgment.

"Surely there was something better for you to do than this?"

"What?" She pulled her hands out of his with an impatient tug. "Name one place where I would fit in." She fingered the amethyst, turquoise and jade velvet pants she wore beneath a lavender-pink cable-knit pullover.

James's gaze swept her, taking in the multihued out-fit and colorful makeup. On any other woman the combination would have been at the very least bizarre. Yet Isis displayed her brilliant plumage with an indescribable grace and elegance. She was breathtaking, sensual and unbelievably bewitching. Unique. One of a kind. She was Isis.

"You can't think of anywhere else either, can you?" she demanded, noting his silence. She leaned back against the seat with a weary sigh. "We'd better get going or it'll be dark by the time we reach my house." She stared out the window, aware that James was watching her but not caring. Once again she had to acknowledge she didn't belong. Not here, not in Egypt, not among her much-loved books. Darn James for making her remember. Usually she kept her feelings of displacement buried in the far recesses of her mind. It was easier to pretend everything was fine in her make-believe world. At least there she looked the part even if she didn't feel it. The muted roar of her car's engine was a welcome interruption to her fruitless mental dialogue. Ironically, she, who provided answers to so many questions of others, had none for herself.

The rest of the trip was passed with little conversation between them. Isis was grateful for James's restraint in dropping the subject of her career. She sensed she had shaken him somewhat with her revelations, although she was unsure how. For her part, she would be glad when she was home.

"Where are you staying?" she asked idly.

"At a small lodge about ten miles from your place," he replied readily as he guided her car through the crowded town streets.

Skiers, snow bunnies and gaily clad children dotted the rustic building-lined thoroughfare of Crystal Bay. Snow lay in cloudy patches of white on the branches of the trees lining Lake Tahoe in the distance. The air was crisp and so incredibly clean it was almost scentless.

"Let me drop my bags in my room, then I'll run you home."

"That's a waste of time. It would be easier for me to leave both you and your luggage and finish the drive myself," Isis got out evenly in spite of a vague twinge of annoyance that surfaced at his self-appointed caretaking role.

She and Josie were due for a very serious talk the moment her friend got back. Her mothering Isis tolerated, even occasionally enjoyed, but for James to treat her like some creature to be pampered—that rankled. Tired she might be, but helpless she was not.

James inclined his head. "If that's the way you want it," he murmured expressionlessly.

He pulled to a halt in the small lot designated for registered guests. Tahoe was well known for its abundance of sports and gambling, but it was equally renowned for its scarcity of parking spaces. Hence most lodgings, even the smaller ones, had carefully marked areas for their patrons' vehicles.

Isis slipped out of the seat to come around to the driver's side. James was waiting, bag in hand. "Thanks for bringing me this far," she offered politely in the awkward silence.

"No problem."

Isis heard the tossed-off comment, yet she couldn't take her eyes from his. The changing depths reflected far more emotion than his neutral tone. "I'm sorry," she breathed without really knowing for what or why she was apologizing.

"Are you?" He lifted his hand to her cheek. "Why?"

The warmth of his fingers was achingly familiar, stirring to life the embers of her awareness of him. "I don't know," she answered honestly, searching his face for a clue to her own ambivalence.

His fingers trailed slowly over her skin to her lips, to trace the full contours with heated roughness. The provocative caress created shivers of anticipation down her spine. The taste of him was a vivid memory, filling her thoughts. She leaned into his touch, barely aware of her actions.

"Isis." His eyes smoldered with latent fire as he stared at her. She was a witch in a woman's form. The feel of her was a narcotic so potent he felt nothing but desire for her, knew no one existed but she. At this moment he wanted, more than the air he breathed, to wrap himself in her softness and strength and forget the world. Tension filled his body at the denial forced upon it. His fingers slipped to her throat and caressed the slender column. He bent his head, unable to resist one kiss, one sip from her delicious mouth to warm him in the lonely center of a black night.

Isis met his lips halfway, every sense alive to this man. Will-o'-the-wisp though he was, he fascinated her beyond anyone she had ever met. She sighed as his mouth covered hers, taking possession in a bold move. The thud of his suitcase when it hit the ground hardly impinged on her consciousness. But the feel of his arms wrapping her did. She caught him close, driven by an urgency he shared.

The sweet duel of their tongues washed waves of desire over her body, drawing her nearer in a vain attempt to eliminate the cloth barrier between them. She moaned softly as his kiss deepened, draining the air from her body and the strength from her legs. His warmth cradled while searing her with a passion so intense it rivaled the sun blazing over the mountaintops.

"James, I want..." Isis began the second her lips were free. Desire coursed through her with such raw power she no longer cared whether they had known each other for minutes or years. This was right. Her every instinct told her so.

"No," he rasped, shaking his head to stem her words. He held her shoulders, too aware of her to put her away from him completely, too aware of his role in her life to allow her to offer herself to him. "We need time, remember. You said so and I agreed. Nothing has changed."

Shocked at his oddly harsh tone, Isis stared at him. He was rejecting her. Why? She felt his arousal, knew it to be as strong as her own, yet he was denying them both.

He shook her once, lightly. "Don't look like that. I don't want this, can't you see?" He glanced around the deserted lot, then back at her face. "I want you. More than I've ever wanted anyone," he admitted huskily. "And because I do, I want the time to be right for us. It's not yet." He lifted his shoulders in an undecipherable shrug.

"Why not now? I'm willing. We're both free. What's the problem?" she demanded, wanting to understand him. "Talk to me, James. Explain the barrier I feel." She hesitated, then continued with painful honesty. "Is it because of my gift? Is that it? Does it worry you?"

"No," he shot back, making no secret of his astonishment. "Whatever gave you such a crazy idea?" He pulled her against his chest, tucking her head beneath his chin. Her uncertainty was a live thing, pulling at him. "I like who you are, what you can do. I even like your bizarre war paint and your rainbow clothes. Any doubts I have have nothing to do with your psychic powers."

"Then what is it?" she mumbled against his throat. She heard his deep sigh with a feeling of frustration.

James closed his eyes against the half-truth he was about to voice. "I want to give us a chance to be sure." And I want to finish this damned assignment without involving you any more than I have, he added silently. His arms tightened around her in an involuntary response to the confession he would have to make in the future. A confrontation that was bound to bring her pain. But a far greater agony lay in wait if he accepted her passion.

"The sun's setting. You should be on your way." He touched his lips to her hair, inhaling the intriguing jasmine scent that clung to the midnight strands.

"I know," Isis agreed without moving. The beat of his heart was a soothing cadence beneath her ear. Dusk encircled them in a benevolent twilight cloak while the breeze from the lake began its cooling caress of the land. She lifted her head to stare at him in the dying light.

"Call me when you get up," he commanded softly.

She nodded, intensely aware of how she wished they could arise together. "It'll be late," she warned quietly. "Even when I'm not working, I'm still a night person."

His teeth shone briefly white as he smiled. "It figures." He bent his head to brush her lips. "Drive carefully, goddess," he murmured against her mouth before taking one final sip from her wine-rich lips. Swift, silent, sure, he took possession completely, returning an equal part of himself before, with a heartfelt groan, he pulled away.

"Goodbye," she whispered as she slipped into the car. He shut the door he'd held open for her.

James stepped back and picked up his discarded suitcase in one smooth motion. For a second their eyes met across the small space separating them. Isis saw the longing she felt reflected in the cloudy depths of his gaze. He was sending her away but the decision was costing him dearly. For a fleeting heartbeat, she rebelled at the waste of his decree. She wanted him—he wanted her. She reached for the door handle.

"No." James's curt order stilled her fingers. He backed up two paces. "Go home, Isis, now. Go home," he repeated roughly, his body tense.

The harshness in his voice restored her sanity in a rush. She straightened with a quick jerk, automatically following his directions. Without another look at him, she reversed the car and eased out of the lot onto the street.

Her hands and eyes obeyed her driving commands despite the chaos of her emotions. The town gave way to the stillness of the open road. Stars flickered on the black heavenly canvas overhead, yet she saw none of it.

He was back there and she was leaving him. It was all wrong, her mind screamed in protest. She should have stayed. But he didn't want that. Time, he said.

"Time," she muttered aloud. "Why do I feel threatened by waiting?" No answer lay either in the emptiness of the road ahead or the cold darkness of the car.

She slowed down to take the right fork leading to her house. The headlights briefly illuminated the sign bearing her name beneath the stylishly lettered Moonlight Oasis. The sensation of homecoming that usually accompanied that particular sight was strangely absent, she realized. The narrow, two-lane passage before her bore to the left up an incline toward the triangular silhouette perched in a clearing on the slope before her. Light glowed a welcome in a multitude of jewel-bright colors through the stained-glass windows on the first floor.

Home. Never had the word seemed so lonely, so bleak. The place she had commissioned and decorated held no appeal. She, who disliked hotel rooms, was drawn more to a small lodge miles away and the man who waited there.

"Time," she breathed, accepting the promise she didn't want. She slipped from the Trans-Am just as the door of a small cottage off to one side opened with a spill of yellow light.

"Welcome back, Isis," Ned called, hurrying across to collect the small overnight case she carried. "You're a little later than I figured."

The familiar voice of Josie's husband and her friend washed over her, dispelling some of the emptiness she felt. She smiled slightly, returning his greeting. "I take it Josie called?" she remarked, following him up the path and into the house.

He nodded vigorously. "Gave me a list of things to do, too," he added with a chuckle. "Lay the fire, turn on the lights, turn back the bed, turn up the thermostat—"

"Enough," she laughed, feeling more at home by the minute. It was impossible to hold her mood with Ned's warmth surrounding her. She unzipped her jacket and hung it on the carved oak coat tree by the door. "Everything looks great." She glanced around appreciatively, noting the cheerful blaze in the natural stone fireplace.

Time was as long or as short as man made it. The idea appeared out of nowhere to lift her spirits further. James wasn't the only one in this twosome with prerogatives. She had some, too.

Six

Isis stretched lazily, her supple body swaying to a soundless melody. Her gaze swept the panoramic view of the lake lying before her. Sun glistened on the dark sapphire surface and blazed a blinding white shower over the snow-shrouded mountains. For a moment she stood in silent appreciation of the vivid scene, before turning to pad across to her bedside phone. The antique gold of her nightgown clung revealingly to her slender form as she perched on the edge of the bed to dial James's number.

He answered on the first ring. "You're early. It's only noon."

Isis focused on the desert painting on the opposite wall as she pictured James in her mind. The faint flicker of amusement in his voice would be mirrored by the tiny, telltale quirk of his lips. "I was asleep early last night," she responded, enjoying her mental image and the banter it inspired. A soft, barely audible indrawn breath indicated the success of her reply.

"How do you feel about skiing?" he asked, changing the subject quickly.

"Like I feel about drowning. Not too impressed," she answered honestly.

James chuckled at her sally. "So that's out," he murmured. "Ice skating?"

"No, I don't know how."

"Gambling?"

"Spectator sport."

He sighed as he ran out of choices. "Your turn."

"How about a horseback ride and a picnic?" she suggested, delightfully wicked ideas forming in her head.

"In December?" James's surprised query slipped out before he could stop it.

Isis ignored his reaction, her enthusiasm rippling in her lightly accented voice. "I've got the horses and by the time you get here, I'll even have a lunch ready for us."

"Early supper," he corrected absently, trying to remember the last time he had been astride anything. Whenever it was, it hadn't been recently and he distinctly recalled that it also hadn't been one of his most shining moments. "I don't ride very well." An understatement to say the least.

Isis hesitated, obviously thinking his comment over. "Not well or not at all?" she asked, having no desire to push him into doing something risky. "We can just have the picnic by itself," she added, some of her excitement ebbing.

James caught her disappointment in the deepening cadence of her tone. Suddenly his memories weren't nearly as important as bringing the lilt back to her voice. "Not well, but I think it's time I improved my ability. You should be a good teacher since you can ride camels and elephants," he teased her in challenge.

"You sure?" she questioned, ignoring his dare in her need for reassurance.

"Just remember to pack a pillow," he returned cheerfully.

He hung up the phone, aware of how out of character his reaction to this woman was. He had spent most of the morning in his room just waiting for her to call. He could have, even should have, used the time to contact his secretary and Nora. He had done neither simply because he wanted to be available the moment she rang. Shaking his head over his own unprecedented behavior, he got to his feet to stare ruefully at the open closet. At least he had some sturdy clothes suitable for the jaunt. It was too bad they weren't padded in certain critical places. This assignment was turning out to be a lot more than he had anticipated, he decided with a philosophical shrug.

It was nearly two hours later by the time he parked his rented car beside Isis's black-and-silver Trans-Am. He sat motionless behind the wheel, momentarily awed by the beauty of the sleekly modern structure soaring gracefully to the sky before him. The simple A-frame echoed the shape of the mountains surrounding it. Yet it was the interesting use of wood, rough stone and the brilliant prisms of stained glass that held his eye.

"You must be Leland."

The gravelly sounding words intruded, snapping him out of his appreciative absorption. He turned to the short older man standing near his car. "I am," he replied briefly before getting out.

Ned inclined his head in a nod of silent greeting. "Isis is around back. She sent me to show you the way." He studied him searchingly. Then he nodded once again, as though satisfied. "I'm Josie's husband, Ned." He held out his work-roughened hand.

James looked first at it, then at the man confronting him. It was evident he had just passed some kind of test. It was equally obvious Ned had a right to make his judgments. Apparently Isis wasn't quite as alone as his report had shown. "I'm James," he stated with an easy handshake.

Ned gestured to the left. "This path will take us to the stables."

James fell into step with his guide, his sharp analytical mind probing the family-type behavior of Ned and Josie; his dossier had stated Isis had no blood kin left. "Have you been with Isis long?"

"About five years, me and the missus."

One brow rose at the short span. From his and Josie's observed actions, he would have guessed a much longer period.

"Yup, she picked us up. Right in the nick of time, too," he added gruffly. "There isn't one thing in this world we wouldn't do for that girl." He halted abruptly, swinging around to study him intently. "We love Isis like she was our own. Josie watches out for her on the road and I take care of here."

James met his eyes steadily. "Does everyone get a warning like this?" he asked, more curious than annoyed at Ned's outspokenness.

"Depends." He glanced toward a small rustic building encircled by a split rail fence. "For all she sees, there's a lot she misses," he explained cryptically.

James followed his gaze just as Isis walked out of the miniature stable leading a shaggy-coated horse. The sunlight shone off the rich ebony of her hair, highlighting the mattresses with gold. Her easy stride and casual attire presented an earthy picture in the primitive setting.

"She's waiting for you." With that Ned left him alone on the trail to return to his cottage.

James barely heard the older man's words as a need as old as life itself surged through him. She was even more bewitching in this guise than in her usual flamboyant display. A smile lifted his lips as she turned and saw him.

Isis caught her breath at the liquid poetry of his movements as he came down the path toward her. That crooked grin warmed her, filling her with happiness. "I was beginning to give you up," she teased when he was within earshot. "It didn't do me one ounce of good to get up early."

James chuckled at her pretended indignation. Her flashing eyes dared him even while they beckoned him nearer. "You didn't say how long it would take you to get ready," he pointed out with a male's logic.

Isis laughed, enjoying his quick reasoning. "No, I guess I didn't. I never do function at my best until late afternoon."

James touched the curve of her cheek with gentle fingers. "Do you know I just realized there is something delightfully decadent about a woman who wears full makeup, including glitzy eye shadow—" he peered at her extravagantly lashed eyes as though making a profound discovery "—along with her work jeans, scuffed boots and orange-plaid flannel shirt."

"Not glitzy," she chided, pleased despite herself at his compliment. "It's incandescent."

"Whatever it is, I like it," he murmured, bending his head until his lips brushed hers. "It hasn't been twenty-four hours yet, and I'm starving for a taste of you."

"Time," Isis breathed, swaying closer. Her body brushed his provocatively. "No playing around, remember."

James caught her pliant form in his arms. "I'm not playing," he rasped, holding her to him, half afraid she would vanish in a puff of smoke. "I've never been more serious."

He captured her mouth, driven by a deep need to claim her as his own. His hands urged her nearer to fuse his strength to her softness. The scent of her rose in his nostrils like a potent aphrodisiac. The power of her allure forced a groan from his lips.

"James," Isis whispered, catching fire in the heat of his passion. Tendrils of desire shot through her. Images of his naked body against her smooth, perfumed skin filled her mind. She arched into his hand as it curled around her breast. His fingers teased the taut peak through her shirt, causing the soft fabric to rub across her sensitive nipple with a delicate roughness.

"You feel so good in my arms, woman," James whispered huskily while trailing kisses across her cheek to the vulnerable nerve below her ear.

Isis shivered in delight when his warm breath feathered over her flesh in the wake of his exploring tongue. "I like what you're doing, but hadn't we better stop?" she asked, while at the same time tipping her chin back to allow him greater access to her neck.

"In a minute. I've been waiting too long to quit now," James answered. He lifted his head fractionally to study her intently. With the voicing of only his needs, his desire ebbed slightly. He wanted to share this pleasure with her, not just take from her. "Strike that. I meant—"

She silenced him with a finger on his lips. She knew without his telling her he regretted the selfish sound of his words. "I know what you mean," she whispered. "I'm right there with you." She wrapped her arms around him, cradling him to her. "You fill up the empty places for me. No one has ever done that before." Her involuntary admission stilled his hands as they began to mold her to him once more.

James froze, staring at the stark truth written in her eyes. Her confession was so close to what he felt, it was uncanny. Reality hovered so near and yet so far. She had never looked more desirable. Maybe he was wrong to deny what they felt. Their need for each other was beyond his assignment. "I want you," he stated deeply, looking into her eyes, hoping to find his passion mirrored there.

Isis exhaled slowly, unaware she had been holding her breath. "And I you." She touched her tongue to her sensitive lips, tasting the faint flavor of him lingering there.

"Are you sure?" It was his turn to silence her with a gesture. "Be sure, Isis. I think neither of us indulges in light affairs. It isn't our way. Once you give yourself to me, once we share ourselves there'll be no going back."

Isis searched his expression, hearing the depth of emotion in his voice and seeing it in his eyes. "I live by my instincts, James. Time never has had any meaning for me. I don't measure my knowledge by ticks of a clock or days on a calendar." She paused, wondering if she was making any sense. How could she explain the feeling of rightness she knew with him? How could she make him understand she had no fear of giving herself?

"What if there are things you don't know about me?" he demanded, wanting to believe in the unreserved offer, but too wary to accept it or her. "Things I can't tell you?"

Isis closed her lashes, hearing the pain in his question. The dark familiar realm of her inner self held the source of her strength and the answer to her doubts. "I know there is a conflict in you. I feel it." Her fingers traced lightly over his features, noting his tense stillness and the anxiety causing it. His physical reactions confirmed what her skilled senses told her.

"Mind reading?" he probed, almost wishing she would discover his secret.

"No," she whispered, still sealed in her dark world. "Never with you unless you ask me to." She opened her eyes to gaze at him. "You more than anyone living are safe from that. Even to protect myself, I would not use you that way."

James inhaled sharply at her solemnly given promise. With her very generosity, she was making herself vulnerable to him. He could and would hurt her. Even if he told the truth now, she would pay for his deception. Later she would pay more. Yet he couldn't put her away from him. He had to go on. He had to believe strengthening their need with passion would make it easier in the end. He knew now noninvolvement would never work. Not for them. Not for the terminally ill woman in New York waiting for the reconciliation with her last remaining family.

"You unman me with your honesty," he murmured, cupping her face with his hands. "If I looked the world over, I have a feeling I would find no other like you. You are a unique lady.'' He brought her close, his lips covering hers in a gentle kiss far removed from the compulsive caresses of earlier.

Isis accepted the almost sexless touch with a small sense of awe. This was a new side of James she had never seen before, a facet that defied description.

He lifted his head, his gaze lightening slowly. "If we're going on that picnic, we should get started," he pointed out softly.

Bemused at the change of subject, Isis made no immediate move to leave his arms. "Picnic?" she echoed as though she had never heard the word. His slow, lopsided smile brought swift comprehension. "Our ride," she exclaimed, disengaging herself with unconscious grace.

She reached up to tuck the few midnight strands escaping the high looped-braid crown atop her head. She gestured toward the horse standing patiently a few feet away. "You get acquainted with Spotty while I get my mount."

James glanced sideways, giving the tall, rough-coated animal an assessing look. "Spotty?" he queried, focusing on the mass of dark brown dots on the well-muscled rump. "That sounds like a dog's name."

Isis dug in her pocket to produce two stubby carrot pieces. "Josie named him," she explained, handing him the vegetable bribe. "He's actually a registered Appaloosa with a long handle no one but a Nez Percé Indian could pronounce."

"Nez Percé?" James held out the orange sticks, absently watching the mare lip up the small offering.

"The tribe that developed these beauties," she said, checking the girth to see that it was snug enough to prevent the saddle from slipping. She patted the dark hide affectionately. "Josie usually rides Spot because Spot has got such a soft mouth and no vices. I promise you'll like her." She chuckled at his skeptical expression. "Hang on till I get Ebony Snow."

James watched Isis's departing figure musingly. Would he ever understand all the complexities of her personality? Her soft, beautifully manicured hands with the shockingly colored nails had handled the saddle with practiced ease. She tossed off equine history unselfconsciously before shooting away with the agility of a gazelle.

A moment later Isis appeared leading a beautiful animal with long legs, wide dark eyes and a snow-white coat liberally sprinkled with uniform black markings. Even to his untutored eye, James could tell he was a champion. But it was the long dark robe vaguely resembling some Arabian sheikh's outfit that Isis now wore that held his attention.

"Like him?" Isis teased, mistakenly interpreting the admiration in James's eyes.

"He's a picture and you know it," he replied automatically while swinging into his saddle. He stifled the urge to catch Isis in his arms and say to hell with their outing. In defense against his primitive impulse, he concentrated on the alert stallion as she mounted. "He's also worth a small fortune, I would guess."

She nodded, her smile peeking at him mischievously as he shifted to a comfortable position. "He is, but more importantly, he's a dependable horse." She gestured toward the wide trail heading into the woods. "We go that way."

James nudged his mount into a swinging walk. "I hope lunch is in these saddlebags," he commented.

"Naturally," she agreed as they entered the ever-green thicket.

Nature closed in around them, shutting out any reminders of the modern world in which they lived. The brief flair of desire at the corral shimmered gently in the quiet. Dormant now, it waited for that one special moment, an unguarded word to give it life once more.

The sounds of bridles jingling, leather creaking and the horses' soft breathing filled the air with images of a more primitive time, further heightening Isis's sensitivity to the man at her side. She inhaled deeply, savoring the crisp cool air entering her body. The simple act was always such a pleasure after the long string of nights performing in smoke-filled lounges.

"You really like it here, don't you?"

She nodded, her eyes a deep sapphire, reflecting her contentment. "It's a home," she stated simply. "Or at least the closest thing I've got to a home." The small tacked-on rider startled her almost as much as it did James.

"Is that dissatisfaction I hear?" He studied her, intrigued by the swift succession of emotions coloring her expression.

She shrugged, hands tightening on the reins just enough to make her horse swerve abruptly. She immediately loosened her hold, then patted Ebony's spotted neck in apology. The small interruption had given her ample time to concoct a glib answer, but oddly, she felt no need for such subterfuge.

"I suppose it is," she admitted, staring straight ahead. "Sometimes I long to roam the world again." She turned slightly in her saddle to snag his gaze. Her brow wrinkled thoughtfully as she tried to explain herself. "I always believed home was a place, I suppose.

We moved so much when I was young, I grew up wanting a settled niche. Then I tried that and discovered I was bored to my back teeth with middle-class convention. So now I roam and come back here when I'm weary." She hesitated, unwilling to express the complete extent of her growing disenchantment.

"Still there's something missing," James hazarded, knowing the feeling well.

Isis nodded, then smiled self-consciously. "Not a very mature attitude at my age, is it?"

"Considering that I've felt the same unrest, I'm not about to agree with that comment." The shade of the trees overhead suddenly gave way to a blindingly white clearing.

Isis reined in, blinking at the shock of the reflected light. "You'd think by now I'd remember to bring sunglasses," she muttered, shielding her eyes with one hand.

James eased his mare over while reaching in his pocket to extract two pairs of glasses. "Here." He handed her one set while he donned the other.

Isis sighed in relief as the silvered screens dispelled the glare. "You wouldn't be psychic, too?" she quipped lightly in an attempt to combat the warmth enfolding her at his protective care.

He shot her a look of unabashed amusement. "Only observant. I noticed you didn't have any eye protection the other day by the lake. With your nocturnal occupation, your sight is probably better geared for artificial light. So putting the facts together..." he said easily.

Isis urged her mount to the fallen tree on the far side. "I think I'd rather stick with my own explanation."

James laughed aloud at her disgruntled comment as he followed her lead. Dismounting, he tied his reins around a convenient branch, then began removing the saddlebags and roll tied to the back of his saddle.

"A tarp?"

Isis glanced over Ebony's withers, one brow raised at his question. "I suppose you'd rather plop down on a soggy blanket?" She waved her hand skyward. "Old Sol there is heating up the white stuff down here, in case you haven't noticed." She tossed her pouches over her shoulder with an unfeminine snort. "Observant?" She sniffed theatrically.

"Do you know your eyes go almost black when you get emotional?" he murmured huskily, his breath feathering heated puffs of air over her cheek.

"Behave," she countered with mock sternness even as her body fit against his with graceful familiarity.

"Why? We're far from the madding crowd. Who's to see?"

Isis turned in his embrace, her bundles dropping unheeded to the ground. The need to move, to touch him was agonizing until she looked into his serious face. Need, desire, hunger, they all lay exposed in his eyes. A lock of brown hair had fallen forward on his forehead, untidily ruffled by their ride. Slowly, feeling as though she had stepped from an ordinary world into a place created just for them, she gently smoothed the strands into place.

Her small caress seemed to work as a catalyst. With a deep groan, James pulled her tight against his body. She cradled his head with her hands, stroking his face softly, offering him the reassurance of her touch.

"Do you know how hard it's been to keep my hands off you, witch?" he moaned. "I need you." He made no move to kiss or caress her. Instead he simply held her, seemingly content to absorb the feel of her into his body.

"I know, James," she whispered. "It seems like I've wanted you forever." She covered his lips with hers, aware as never before of how much she wanted to share with this man.

He pulled away a fraction of an inch to study her intently. "You do pick your moments." He closed his eyes, sighing deeply. "I wish we had a private place, a bed and a long night."

Holding his face in her hands, Isis smoothed the troubled lines from his brow with gentle strokes and a softly whispered kiss on his lips. "We have all that here," she murmured. "Everything except the night. Will an afternoon do?"

At her words, James's lashes snapped open in unfeigned amazement. "Here?" he demanded, staring first at her, then around the small deserted clearing. "In the snow?"

Isis nodded, her eyes glistening deeply blue to match the woman-wise smile on her lips. She stepped back to loosen the silver-tassled tie from around her royal-purple robe.

James watched in puzzlement as she took off the flowing garment, then picked up the bundled tarp lying at their feet. He followed her to a cloudy, melting snowdrift piled near a small ridge at the edge of the open space. In seconds her deft movements produced a contoured couch just big enough for two.

"Snow and desert sand are not so very different," she said, sinking down onto the pallet she had made for them. "The sun is warm, the canvas will keep us dry and this—" she touched her coat lightly, her eyes inviting him to join her "—is as soft as any sheet."

James stood motionless, caught by her words and her openly sensual approach. She offered him no guileful tricks, no silly woman games, no maidenly protests. Her actions were honest, straightforward, but contained an innate feminine allure made all the more powerful for its lack of artifice. He knelt slowly down before her, his hands covering her. One at a time, he lifted them to his lips, his gaze never leaving hers. "If ever I had a fantasy, you would be mine."

Seven

Not fantasy, reality,'' Isis breathed as she lay back and held out her arms to him.

His eyes flared with fierce emotion as he accepted the silent invitation. He gathered her close, to trail warm kisses over her face and throat. One hand slid upward to cup her breast beneath the soft flannel shirt. She moaned in pleasure with his touch, arching into him.

Restlessly her hands kneaded his muscled shoulders to slip down his chest to the buttons of his shirt. Her fingers agilely worked the fastenings, finishing their task almost at the same second he parted her blouse. The cool whisper of air over her skin was an erotic brush of sensation against her passion-sensitive nipples. Tension coiled slowly in the center of her being, lifting her toward the source of her rising need.

Clothes seemed to float magically away from their bodies as their desire for each other grew. James caressed and shaped her curves with a beautiful absorption so complete Isis knew no other touch, sound or feel but his. With infinite patience and tenderness he learned about her as though this would be his one and only chance in all of eternity.

Driven by the same urgency, Isis explored him, this man, her lover. With him, everything was sunrise fresh and golden. Angles, lean planes, corded muscles were all special places to be caressed, touched and stroked. She bent her head, her lips tracing a path across his ribs in the wake of her adventurous fingers.

His chest rose and fell rapidly beneath her touch, his harsh breathing a primitive rhythm in her ear. "Don't stop," he rasped as her hands slipped down his stomach and beyond.

Lying beside him, Isis felt the rigid desire in her palm, knowing as never before a sense of awe at her own power. To be wanted so much by him was intoxicating and bewitching at one and the same time. "Man was perfectly created for woman," she breathed huskily. She drew long, tantalizing sweeps over his hips and inner thighs. "Every part of you pleases me."

James shivered with each new caress. His hands on her body mirrored Isis's movements. "Temptress," he growled, catching her in his arms to roll her over on her back. His hands caught hers, lifting them over her head to be held there by one fist. "I'm going up in flames wanting you."

He bent his head to her breasts to encircle the tight buds awaiting his possession. Isis arched into his mouth, enjoying his gentle mastery. She quivered as white heat filled her body, driving her ever closer to the unbearable point of desperate need.

With growing urgency, he lavished her body with hungry, claiming kisses. His caresses slid lower over her undulating belly to the dark curls beyond.

Isis gasped aloud when he reached the pulsating center of her desire. Eyes wide, she lifted her body in eager demand. Splintering, aching pleasure built within her. But there was emptiness, too. A sweet void only he could fill.

"James." Her call was a demand as old as life itself. A plea as young as her next breath.

James rose in answer while at the same moment releasing her hands. Her arms slipped around his neck as she welcomed him into her embrace. He hesitated for a moment, savoring their joining. Then he began to move, slowly, deeply.

Isis caught her breath at the exquisitely pleasuring pace. Every sense was alive, every part of her fusing with him to create a world beyond reality. Stars—heat—light—tension—sound— "James."

"Isis."

Twin cries of complete ecstasy echoed in their winter-forest mating place. His mouth found hers in that heart-stopping moment, sealing their union with a kiss of deep, unbounded tenderness.

Long minutes passed as time righted itself. Isis opened her lashes to gaze directly into the warm hazel depths of James's eyes. "Still think that was fantasy?" she whispered with a lover's teasing.

"Reality," he murmured, tucking her more securely against his side. "You were right about this spot, too."

Isis wriggled enticingly. "I'll bet you thought it would be cold," she purred, lightly scoring his chest with her nails.

The warmth of the sun on her back was pleasant, but his body heat was even more so. The fluffy cloud of snow under them was softer than the most expensive bedding. She had never felt more content or complete. She drew the edges of the robe over them, enclosing them in a downy cocoon. Long, silent minutes ticked by as they lay entwined together without speaking.

With each breath she took, Isis inhaled James's heady scent. His every movement rippled through her as though they were one. "I suppose we should eat now," she suggested languidly.

"Probably," he agreed, making no immediate effort to release her. He dropped a kiss on her forehead before tipping her chin up so he could see her expression. "You didn't have breakfast, did you?"

"No," she admitted. The storm clouds gathering in his eyes brought a hint of tension to her body. "Now don't start that again."

James ran his hand down the lithe contours of her form until his fingers rested on the curve of her too slender hip. "Woman, much as I like your figure, I'd rather see a few more pounds here and there." He sat up, lifting her with him. He tossed back their purple covering, rose and pulled her to her feet.

Isis stared at him, finding it difficult to believe he was really serious. One look at his determined face and brisk, efficient movements as he dressed convinced her he was. "When I get my hands on that Josie," she muttered while she began putting on the clothes James tossed at her.

"You'll thank her for caring," he finished sternly, his gaze following her unconsciously provocative actions with male appreciation. "Besides, if you weren't so unconcerned about your own health, no one would need to worry about you."

"It might surprise you to know I've survived quite a while without either you or Josie nagging at me," she countered. She tugged on her last boot and stood up, hands on her hips. "I'm thirty-two, not three."

James chuckled at her belligerent stance, his eyes gleaming with wicked knowledge. "Honey, I know very well you're a woman, not a child. I enjoy you and your sexy body but—" he frowned while he leaned down to pick up the forgotten saddlebags "—I intend to see that you take care of yourself when I'm around." He straightened, giving her a no-nonsense stare.

Isis's lips parted soundlessly at the unexpected steel in his expression. "And I thought you were a nice harmless male when I met you," she grumbled, plunking down on their bed-now-picnic-mat. "You remind me of a king cobra with the way you change personalities. It looks perfectly ordinary, too, until it spreads its hood and rears back to strike."

At her words, James hesitated imperceptibly. How quick she was to catch every tiny nuance. If he wasn't careful, she'd start questioning him about his past, maybe even his work. He couldn't have that, not because he couldn't make up a plausible story, but because he hated to lie any more than he had to. Better to play it light, he reminded himself as he forced his muscles to relax. Make it a joke.

James knelt before her, his eyes dancing with amusement. "I should have known you'd choose something as offbeat as a snake to compare me with," he observed easily. "Has it occurred to you my so-called changes are a direct result of yours?" He opened each of the pouches with every appearance of being absorbed in the contents.

Isis moved to help him. "I've never been as erratic as you are. And nobody would describe me as nice. Garish or theatrical, perhaps, but definitely not nice." She ignored his choke of laughter when he tossed the last empty saddlebag aside. She scanned the assorted containers and packages between them, her brow wrinkled in puzzlement. "I know I didn't wrap up two things of chicken." She poked one plum-colored fingernail at a plastic bag filled with assorted desserts. "And unless this jumped in by itself, I didn't pack it either. Two brownies, two Dutch apple squares, two fried cherry pies. Ned! I swear I'll wring his neck," she vowed ruefully. She opened the pastries and extracted one dark square. She took a bite, then grinned. "Although on second thought..."

James laughed, plucking the pilfered goodies from her fingers. "Saved by a brownie, is he?" He handed her a plate. "Fill it up," he ordered with a crooked grin.

With her mouth full of her fudgy treat and eyes dancing with amusement, Isis obeyed his directive without protest. Moments later they were munching companionably and exchanging background information about themselves. Isis learned James had grown up in a small town in Missouri and that he had two brothers, one older and one younger. Both his parents were still living. He had become interested in gems at an early age when helping his father in the family jewelry store.

"All very ordinary middle class," he confessed with a smile that laughed at his roots while respecting them, too. He helped her gather together the remnants of their picnic.

"Ordinary is in the mind of the one familiar with it," Isis shrugged. "Your life seems very exotic to me. A mother at home, baking cookies, a school with friends who all spoke the same language, literally, picnics like this, football games." She paused to stare out at the lake. "Something as simple as this setting is new to me."

His eyes softened at the loneliness he heard in her voice. He touched her shoulder, his fingers curving around the delicate bones covered in flannel. It was the first time he had done more than accidentally brush against her since they had made love. "Why didn't you go back?" he asked gently.

Without turning her head, Isis leaned her cheek against his hand. "I needed to go to college and I knew my father wanted me to come back to the States to do it." She sighed, absently noting the silvery glints of sunlight against the sapphire mirror of the lake. "Besides, with him gone I really had no reason to stay in Egypt."

"That must have been hard for you. To bury him there, then come halfway around the world to a country you barely knew."

Isis did look at him then. The understanding and sympathy in his hazel gaze enfolded her like a warm blanket. How easy it was to talk to him. As close as Ned and Josie were, even they didn't realize the upheaval she had gone through all those years ago. "I survived," she murmured quietly. She lifted her hands in a foreign gesture of acceptance. *"In sha allah."*

James cocked his head, his expression curious. "What does it mean?"

"As God wills. It's an Arabic expression—courtesy of my father's assistant, Ahmed."

"In sha allah," James repeated without faltering. His exact inflection and pronunciation drew an admiring glance.

"It sounds like you're no stranger to languages." Isis studied him speculatively. "You never did tell me exactly what you do. I know you're here to see Metcalf about a necklace..." Her voice trailed away, inviting him to explain himself.

"I find things for people," he offered with deliberate ambiguity. "My work takes me into quite a few places where English isn't the predominant tongue." He closed the last saddlebag and sat back on his heels. He met her eyes, knowing he dared show no hesitation or evasiveness. Her perception was a formidable truth-finding tool.

"So you find the rare for those who appreciate the unusual. A strange occupation for a jeweler's son from Missouri."

"Perhaps," he agreed, breathing a mental sigh of relief. He hadn't lied. And she seemed satisfied with his answers. He rose and collected their pouches.

"So what about Burt Metcalf? Did you ever get together with him?" she asked, making no effort to get up.

James straightened slowly, his gaze locking on her. "No, after our contretemps the other night, I didn't think it advisable."

"Why?" she queried, feeling something alien intrude in the peaceful clearing. There was a fine tension in the barely perceptible control of his movements.

Here, at least, he could be honest. "He may not be receptive to parting with what I've come to get," he admitted carefully. "I had hoped to approach him in a pleasant nonbusiness setting first, but it didn't work out that way. Now I have to figure out another method of seeing him."

Isis frowned at the twinge of guilt his answer brought. It was because of her he had gotten off on the wrong foot with Metcalf. "I wish there were some way I could help you," she remarked, thinking aloud.

Once again she had provided him with the opportunity he sought. He had to take it. He couldn't afford to pass up this chance as much as one part of him would like to. "Well, if you had accepted his invitation, I could go along with you," he tossed out casually. He shrugged as though dismissing the possibility. He held out his hand. "It's getting close to sundown. We'd better go," he suggested, changing the subject. How he hated this role of manipulator. Damn Nora's illness, the Sapphire Shower and the trust he had to abuse to help an old friend right a wrong. If only he could explain.

Lost in thought, Isis placed her fingers in his to allow him to pull her to her feet. She started slightly when he slipped his arm around her waist and hugged her to him.

"Stop worrying, honey, I'll work it out," he commanded huskily.

"I could call him," she murmured, staring into his fog-shrouded eyes.

"No," he disagreed, forgetting his role in his dislike of having her approach the older man. The image of her pale, strained face when he had found Metcalf in her dressing room haunted him. She had been so exhausted, so in need of care, not someone demanding more of her fragile strength.

"But James," Isis protested, only to be silenced by his lips.

His kiss was a gentle thing, no real pressure or passion, only a quiet warmth invading her being. Then it was gone, over almost before it had begun, and with it her continued arguments.

"No more, woman. This is our time," he decreed. The seeds were planted. Perhaps they would bear fruit. If not, he would work something else out. He tucked her against his side and headed for the horses.

"The tarp and my robe," Isis reminded him, wiggling out of his embrace to go back. She quickly slipped into her long desert garment, then efficiently rolled the canvas into a neat bundle.

"Why didn't you wear your hair down?" he asked suddenly as she came toward him.

"I don't know," she replied when she stopped beside him. "I just didn't think of it."

He touched the thick braid at the top of her head. The shiny glint of black pins against the dark strands reminded him of the heaviness they held. One by one, he removed the metal objects until the single plait uncoiled like a live creature and swung down Isis's back.

"Why did you do that?" she asked, watching the concentration mirrored in his expression with fascination.

"Turn around," he murmured, ignoring her question.

Surprised and curious, Isis did as he requested. "Without that braid, I have a horse's mane with a mind of its own," she warned, when she felt him release the tie that secured the long rope.

"If it tangles, I'll brush it for you," he offered huskily. He lifted the half-braided swath to his face, inhaling its spicy floral scent. "It's too beautiful to keep chained up." He bent his head to drop a kiss below her ear.

Isis shivered pleasurably at his light caress. When the tip of his tongue moved intimately, learning every contour of her ear, she made an inarticulate sound. She barely noticed that he finished unwinding the rest of her hair as she tilted her head to allow him greater access to her neck. His lips trailed a path of moist heat down the side of her throat, his tongue flicking expertly beneath her collar to the tender skin it protected.

"James," she whispered, turning toward him while at the same time dropping her burden.

"Isis," he breathed deeply, his eyes roving boldly over her unusual features. She was a flame of desire in his core; she was a mystery he wanted to solve, a treasure he had to possess. Once was not enough. "Let's go home. I need you."

Isis nodded, too lost in the sensual web he spun to give voice to words. He put her gently away from him, his eyes betraying reluctance to let her go. For a second, her fingers clung to his shoulders, refusing to break the last physical tie.

"Now, Isis, behave or we'll stay and freeze in each other's arms." He lifted her hands from his body, squeezed them briefly, then released her. He turned and walked swiftly to his mare to snap on the saddlebags.

Isis moved to Ebony's side, tied on the tarp after fixing her pouches in place. Moments later, they were trotting side by side back the way they had come.

It was a silent ride, full of unspoken closeness. His thigh brushed hers, lingering for a minute to draw her eyes to his. His gaze caressed her body, skimming her flowing garment with deliberate intent to arouse and excite. Even the ordinary motion of her stallion's long reaching gait as he stretched into an easy canter heightened her desire. The rocking brought to mind the intimate memory of James's body plunging into hers. The heat of her body mingled with his scent still clung to her robe to further heighten the strange surrealistic imagery.

Needing to regain control of her wayward senses, Isis forced the vivid recollections out of her mind. Instead, she concentrated on the tall evergreens laced with snow lining their path, the play of sunlight through the branches, anything but the memory of James's lovemaking.

"At last," James said feelingly, when together they emerged from the trees. The corral, the barn and Isis's house on the hill lay before them.

Isis glanced at him as she drew her mount to a cooling walk. "Saddle sore?" she asked, raising one brow in amused inquiry. Mentally she blessed her years of self-discipline for the steadiness of her voice.

James grimaced while shifting position to accommodate the change in gait. "A hot tub would go a long way to making me feel more human," he admitted bluntly.

"Would you settle for a spa?"

His eyes lit up with enthusiasm. "For that I just might make it off this horse and up to wherever it is before I collapse."

Isis laughed, although her expression managed to be suitably sympathetic. In spite of James's grumbling, she could tell he wasn't in quite as bad shape as he pretended. "You mean I'm going to be stuck with unsaddling your horse and mine, too?" She clucked her tongue chidingly as she leaned over to open, then close after them the gate into the corral.

"I'm not too proud to accept your help," he shot back with a grin. "If the saddle were on the other rear, I'd offer to do yours."

At his mangled quote, Isis came erect to stare at him. "That's terrible," she pointed out after a moment's consideration.

"Possibly, but you'll have to agree it's apt," he countered with mock innocence.

Isis drew her Appaloosa to a halt, dismounting with ease. She determinedly ignored James's pained groans as he copied her actions. "No work, no reward," she decreed as she loosened Ebony's girth.

"I never would have said you were a tough lady," James mumbled, enjoying their banter to the hilt. He removed the mare's saddle and tossed it over the top rail of the fence. "Where's Ned?" He turned just in time to accept the currycomb, brush and towel Isis held out to him.

"By now he should be with Josie." She smoothed her cloth over the damp patch on Ebony's back where the saddle had rested. "He'll be staying overnight for dinner and a little gambling, then they'll come back together in the morning."

James's hand stilled, the brush suspended above the shaggy coat he was grooming. "You'll be alone here?"

She glanced up, caught by the subtle question hidden in his query. For a split second she hesitated at admitting the desire burning within her. Then with a mental shrug, she decided the honesty she had always valued was the best course.

"Not if you stay with me," she invited quietly. Her eyes held his, knowing he could see her need for him mirrored there. His slow smile lifted the right corner of his mouth before spreading over his lips to light his gaze. Longing to match her own shone in the illuminated depths.

"Is that spa big enough for two?" he demanded after a short but telling pause.

"I don't know. I've never tried it before," she replied softly. She held her breath as he took a step around his horse toward her, then stopped.

"Let's get a move on, woman. I have an ache that's screaming for a hot tub," he commanded huskily.

He wasn't the only one with an ache, Isis added silently as she efficiently finished Ebony's rubdown. But would one night, any more than one union, be enough? Or would a second taste of him only aggravate her hunger as the first had done?

Eight

——

You weren't kidding," James murmured as Isis opened French doors onto a glass-enclosed patio.

Outside, snow-layered trees dotted the white landscape in the twilight of evening. But inside it was warm with the scent of growing plants. Smooth cedar floors and comfortable padded furniture created a relaxing atmosphere. The spa itself was set in a raised platform at one end beneath a duo of oversized skylights.

"Like it?" Isis asked as his silence lengthened.

"Who wouldn't?" he replied dryly, his gaze focused on the bare windows. "I suppose the glass is coated for privacy?" He glanced at her, one brow raised to punctuate his question.

She nodded while reaching for the light switch. "When these are off, we might as well be behind solid walls." A muted click shrouded the room in velvety darkness. It took a moment for her eyes to adjust to the natural illumination before she could see James clearly.

He closed the distance between them until he could touch her face. "Your house is as unique as you are," he murmured softly, his fingers tracing lightly over her jaw to her throat. "Everywhere I look, I see color and life. There are hardly any walls except the outer ones."

"I wanted it that way," she breathed, caught in the seductive mood he spun. His words could hardly have been more ordinary. But they, like the man who spoke them, were much more than what they seemed. "I need space; I always have."

"So do I," he agreed, stroking her golden throat gently. His hand dipped lazily down to the V at the top of her shirt. His thumb strayed intimately under the snap fasteners to nestle in the snug harbor between her breasts.

Isis could have stayed that way all night and been content, if she could have ignored the smoldering desire heating her blood. "James."

She barely had time to breathe his name before his lips closed on hers in a kiss that seared through her with the force of lightning. His hard body pressed against her softness, making her aware of every vibrant muscle and sinew.

"You're just made for me," he groaned as he slid one hand under her hair to cradle her head for his kiss.

Isis slipped her arms around his neck, vaguely aware of the miniature chain of snaps that bared her breasts for his touch. His hands on her were just as eager as her own to rediscover the tactile delight awaiting them.

The expression in his eyes when he lifted his head was rich with passionate intensity. His fingers glided lightly over her firm belly, teasingly outlining the waist of her jeans. "You have too many clothes on," he muttered hoarsely.

"So do you," she whispered in turn. She caught an edge of his shirt in each hand and gave one swift pull. The western fasteners parted easily to reveal the long length of his tanned chest.

Reluctantly James stepped back to shrug out of his shirt while Isis did the same. Their eyes met and held when, as one, their fingers went to their belts to remove their jeans. He was all clean lines and compact rippling muscles to her gentle curves and delicately fashioned hips and breasts. He reached out to cup one taut globe in his palm, his face tight with need. He bent his head slowly to take the dusky nipple in his mouth.

At the touch of his lips on her skin, Isis arched to him. Moaning deep in her throat, she buried her face against his neck as he caressed her breasts with his hands. His tormenting lips moved down to the smooth swell of her belly and he tongued her navel with light, sensuous strokes until she writhed in his embrace.

With a low groan of satisfaction, he gathered her in his arms and strode swiftly up the spa platform, then down into the hot swirling water.

Isis gasped as she was enveloped in the silken heat. He cradled her securely astride him as he sat on the seat beneath the water. "Here?" she questioned, the aching need he had created clear in her voice.

"Here," he agreed with a masculine look of challenge. Then his body was surging against hers as he held her firmly in place.

The primitive rhythm was slowed and somehow intensified by the slight resistence offered by the water. It created an incredibly languid, erotic sensation that seemed to complement the white hot desire driving them.

Slowly at first, then with increasing urgency, Isis caught the pattern of James's movements. Her body responded as it always had to his power, adapting eagerly to the aquatic environment.

"Isis," he gasped, his hands clenched tightly into her hips as he guided their mating dance. "My woman."

His were the last coherent words either of them spoke. Primordial sounds rose in a male-female melody to harmonize with timeless lap of the waves against their plunging bodies. Faster and faster surged the sea surrounding them, hurtling them ever closer to fulfillment.

Isis cried out, clinging to James with all her strength as her body trembled. She tumbled headlong in a cascade of blazing passion. Deliriously, she gave herself up to the support of James's arms as he quivered against her in his own release.

They lay quiescent for a long time after in the swirling froth. Content, replete, Isis left the problem of flotation to her lover. She trusted James, she realized in some dim portion of her mind. He would take care of her. She felt his fingers stroking her back when she nestled against his chest.

"You didn't think we could do it," he teased affectionately, reminding her of her surprise at his choice of a loving place.

"No," she agreed, too lazy to argue.

He laughed, a sound she felt rumble deep in his chest. "Such docility. I have a feeling I'd better treasure this moment..."

The soft mood was rudely interrupted by the shrill ringing of the phone across the patio.

"Blast," she grumbled, eyeing the demanding instrument with dislike. She reluctantly pushed away from his body. "Of all the times for it to ring."

"Leave it," he commanded, his hand sliding intimately down her form.

"Can't," she muttered, rising in the bubbling water to stand in glistening perfection before him. "That's my unlisted line. Very few people besides Ned and Josie have the number."

Sighing his acceptance of her reasons, he stood to follow her out of the tub. Isis padded across the floor to a decorative stand surrounded by potted ferns. Bending down, she pulled out two large, scarlet bath sheets. She wrapped one around her dripping curves and handed the other to him. The phone continued to demand attention with a seventh ring before Isis picked it up.

Her eyes widened in surprise on hearing the impatient male voice on the other end.

"Mr. Metcalf," she said neutrally in greeting.

On hearing the identity of her caller, James paused in the act of drying himself. The sense of well-being that had filled him in the wake of their lovemaking gave way to alertness.

"No, I'm sorry. I explained before. I no longer do private shows." Isis held the phone away from her ear slightly as Burt loudly expressed his dissatisfaction. She glanced at James to find him watching her intently. Suddenly the words he had spoken earlier about his reason for being in Nevada came to her mind. Because of her he had sacrificed one meeting with the reclusive owner of the Midnight Sun. Now it was within her power to help him. Her thoughts raced to find a solution without giving up her rules.

The rough voice growled her name. She put the receiver back in place just in time to hear the new spate of arguments. She listened, her gaze no longer focused on James. Instead, she was turning a solution over in her mind.

"No, the money's not the issue. Yes, I know what a recommendation from you could do for my career." She shook her head while stamping down on her annoyance at his persistence. "Mr. Metcalf," she interrupted ruthlessly, knowing no other way to stem the flow of words. "How about a bargain? You want me to perform at a large Christmas party for..." She named a sum nearly three times her usual fee for a two-night engagement.

James sucked in a breath at the figure, while absently noting how offhand Isis was with it. Nothing in her expression showed appreciation of the amount. But even that revelation lost its importance in the offer of a compromise. Had she decided to help him? He listened closely, masking his eagerness behind a shield of calm inquiry.

"Yes, I understand how much it means to Mrs. Metcalf. Certainly I sympathize with her psychic interest. That's exactly why I thought I would offer to come down one day next week. Your wife and I could talk, I could do a little work and answer her questions. Surely that would be much more interesting for her than just watching my act. After all, you two sat through it for four nights in a row."

There was silence on the other end of the line as Metcalf turned her proposal over in his mind. Isis lifted her eyes to James's face, her lips curving into a conspiratorial smile. She could feel her opponent weakening.

"Not one day, the weekend," Metcalf countered, making a bargain of his own. "I'll send my car for you."

"No, I'll drive myself." She hesitated. This was the tricky part. "May I bring a friend?" She gave James a thumbs-up sign.

"If you wish," he replied tersely. "See you Friday afternoon."

Isis grimaced at his abrupt ending of the conversation as she hung up the phone.

"Did I hear right?" James asked carefully. "Did you just get us invited to his estate?"

She nodded jauntily, satisfaction and triumph in every line of her body as she strolled toward him.

"I owed you one for protecting me the other night. And I always pay my debts."

James caught her bare shoulders when she stopped in front of him. His eyes impaled her with sudden ferocity. "You don't owe me one damned thing," he bit out. Self-disgust at the way he was using her made his voice harsher than he intended.

Isis tipped her head, feeling the waves of anger pour over her without understanding the cause. "I thought you'd be pleased," she murmured, studying him with grave attention.

"I am," he agreed immediately. "More than I can possibly explain to you. The Sapphire Shower that Metcalf has is very important to my client." He pulled her to him, cradling her body against his with a tenderness he couldn't deny. "I don't like having to involve you in my job."

Isis's eyes clouded as she sifted through the conflicting emotions she sensed in him. The tension in his body bespoke his anger, yet his hold was so gentle she knew only a feeling of security and protection.

"You didn't involve me," she argued, knowing no other way to reassure him. "I chose to help you if I could."

James shut his eyes against the generosity of her answer. Mentally he damned the circumstances forcing him into this role. Isis was a woman made for honesty. She gave of herself freely. She deserved only the best of him in return.

And he wanted to give her the world at her feet, he acknowledged silently. He needed her in his arms and in his life. He wanted to hold her, protect her from every hurt. Yet he could not, for his was the biggest hurt of all.

He had had to lie to her. His arms tightened on her towel-wrapped form. Would she listen to him when he was finally free to explain? Would he even have the right to ask her to?

"James?" Isis touched his face, lightly tracing the deceptively strong bone structure. "Something's wrong; I can feel it. Tell me what it is. Maybe I can help."

James opened his eyes at her hushed speaking of his name. The worry, the compassion in her gaze flowed over him bringing relief mixed with pain. "If anyone could, it would be you, but this is something I must handle alone."

He bent his head to taste her lips. He had never needed her more than he did at this moment. He crushed her to him, inhaling the fresh woman scent of her. At least this was without the taint of his lies. This fire in his blood he could offer her freely. She was his woman, unlike any he had ever known. His desire for her was alive and new, untouched by the subterfuge of the present. He lifted her into his arms, his eyes sweeping over her supple grace possessively.

"Will you share your bed with me?"

Isis touched his lips with her fingertips. Her eyes shimmered with a liquid radiance in the silvery moonlight pouring through the windows. "Yes, please," she whispered huskily as she nestled still closer to his hard warmth.

It was midmorning when Isis languidly opened her eyes. Bright sunlight streamed through the floor-to-ceiling windows leading to her second-floor deck. She raised a hand to push back her tumbled hair, a sleepy though decidedly wicked smile curving her lips.

"I knew you'd look delicious when you woke up," James murmured, gazing at her tenderly.

Isis caught her breath in wonder as she stared at him. He was completely dressed, hair still damp from a recent shower. He sat on the edge of the bed as if he had been there a long time.

"It's rude to stare at someone when they're asleep," she reproved in a breathy rush, her faint accent slightly more noticeable than usual. He looked so right sitting there, she thought in vague surprise. Strong, intensely male, he seemed to fit well with the rich color of her royal-purple, silver and cream bedroom.

"I like to look at you," he confessed with a faint smile. He bent his head to kiss her gently. "I also like to touch you."

He nuzzled her neck. His early morning beard rasped pleasantly over her skin, sending light chills down her spine. "Your skin is soft and warm." He inhaled deeply. "Your scent fills my mind." He drew back reluctantly, changing the subject quickly. "Your coffee's getting cold." He leaned across to lift a cup and saucer from the ornately carved bedside table.

Blinking at the swift insertion of the mundane, Isis sat up in bed, banking the pillows behind her. She tucked the sheet around, feeling oddly pampered by him. It was such a switch from James the lover. That James had taken intense sensual pleasure in memorizing every inch of her body in the wild, passionate hours of the night. She accepted his offering, her eyes on his.

"Aren't you having any?" she asked before taking a sip of the perfectly brewed liquid.

He shook his head. "I thought I'd better dress and take off before your friends get back." He hesitated, frowning at the stark sound of his words. He was thinking of her, not of himself.

Isis's lashes dropped to hide her disappointment. She had wanted to wake up in his arms. "I suppose it would be best," she admitted on a sigh.

James lifted her chin, his gaze warm on her sleep softened features. "I don't like leaving you, honey. But I'd hate embarrassing you or making you uncomfortable in front of your protectors even more." He outlined the curve of her lower lip with the tip of his finger. "Can you understand that?"

Isis felt an aching lump in her throat at his perception. For the first time in her life she felt like crying. "Yes," she whispered.

"Have dinner with me tonight," he coaxed, clearly displaying his desire for her company.

"I'd like that," she answered simply, her eyes glowing with pleasure at his suggestion. Already she was missing him and he hadn't left her yet.

He withdrew his hand, his gaze openly caressing her. For a long moment neither spoke as their eyes met and held. It would be so easy to accept the slumberous invitation in Isis's eyes, to bury himself in her body and never count tomorrow. But he resisted his needs. He had remembered his job too well this morning when he had awakened with her curled trustingly against him.

Her life-style and her friends were important to her. His report had told him so and she had confirmed his findings. He could never regret loving her but he refused to disrupt her life any more than he had. He had taken so much, returned so little; surely this, at least, he could give her.

He shook his head, clearing his thoughts before getting to his feet. "Is seven all right?"

Isis nodded, wanting him to kiss her more than she had ever needed anything before. She almost reached out to him but something stopped her. She curled her nails into her palms as she fought back the urge. "Yes, seven will be fine," she agreed quietly.

She watched silently as he inclined his head once, then walked out of the bedroom. She listened to his measured footsteps on the cedar treads of the stairs as he left her. It had to be the loneliest sound she had ever heard. She wanted to call him back, to hold him in her arms again.

Suddenly, uncaring of her nudity, she tossed back the covers and got up to stride to the windows. The protective glazing hid her from view but allowed her an unrestricted look at the parking area set at the bottom of the hill. She tensed as James appeared on the path. Her gaze flowed over him, remembering their passion of the night. He stopped, turned and stared up to where she stood.

A heartbeat, two, then three and he was moving away again. Faster this time as though their parting was as painful for him as it was for her. She watched him go until even his car had disappeared from sight. Sighing, she padded back to the bed. She stopped, studying the rumpled emptiness of the lavender sheets.

So much had happened in so little time, yet hadn't her life always been so? She had never known such an intense attraction to a man. He had been so ordinary looking, so completely unassuming, but still she had felt a pull of something beyond what she could see. Not psychic exactly, more of an affinity, a recognition of kindred feelings.

She touched her now-cold cup of coffee. And James? He had entered her life as though he belonged, badgering her about her eating habits with more success than the redoubtable Josie. He showed his care of her in many ways more familiar than those of longtime associates.

A smile curved her lips, as she remembered their picnic when they had shared their bodies and their minds. It had been so easy to talk to him, to tell him things she rarely told anyone else. Was that why she was feeling this pain of separation? The depth of reaction was startling. She had always known James meant much more than a casual fling, but this...this what? Love?

She frowned, examining the word as though it were an intruder. So little time. Could love grow out of so little? No, her mind concluded vehemently, but her heart and the extraordinary sense she possessed quietly said it was so. She inhaled deeply, then let her breath go on a long sigh filled with self-knowledge.

She loved James. She had given him the gift of her body, so now it would seem she had given him her heart, too. Her lips curved upward in a secretive woman

smile. Her first love. How could she make it her last?
Did James love her? Could he come to love her?

"So many questions," she murmured softly. "How
I wish I could read his mind." Never had she regretted
her vow more. She needed the reassurance of knowing
his feelings. Yet even with this uncertainty, she could
not sacrifice her integrity. Her life was built on honesty. She had no use for lies.

Nine

———

Sleep well, goddess,'' James whispered huskily, his fingers trailing lightly over her silk-covered breasts.

Isis arched longingly into the tantalizing caress. Less than two hours ago, she had lain in his arms, lost to the world in a passionate storm of his creating. And now, as every night for the past three evenings, he was leaving her at her door.

"Why didn't you let me stay with you?" she questioned throatily, repeating a demand she had made more than once. "I wanted to."

James's arms tightened around her, momentarily crushing her pliant body against his tougher frame. "Soon, honey, I promise."

Isis lifted her head from his shoulder. "When?" she countered, the frustration she felt at his attitude tinging her tone. The tension in his body communicated itself to her almost instantly. "Tell me, James," she insisted, feeling him withdraw and unable to stop him. "Every time I ask to do more than warm your bed, you pull away. What is it?"

James stared at her, seeing the pain and uncertainty in her eyes. "I want to tell you," he admitted.

"So there is something," Isis breathed, relieved and apprehensive at the same time. She searched his face, looking for the smallest clue.

"Give me until Monday," he half asked, half pleaded.

"After we come back from Metcalf's," she clarified slowly.

He nodded. "I'll explain everything, I promise."

Isis hesitated, aware of the questions plaguing her. The most notable one was why after this particular weekend? Surely a possible meeting over a piece of jewelry had no bearing on their relationship.

"Monday," she agreed finally, working solely on the belief she had in him. Her mind argued reservations, but her instincts and her love demanded trust. No man could make love to a woman the way he did without feeling something special.

The rigidity drained out of James's body at her words; his eyes deepened to a rich jade smoke at her generosity. Let me make this right for her, he begged whatever hand ruled the universe. He lowered his head to capture her lips in a kiss that betrayed his desperation and need.

Instantly, Isis responded to his demand, as desire barely held in check blazed out of control. She clung to him, her fingers spearing through his hair in an effort to bring him closer. Tongues dueled in a heated battle to explore the territory each guarded. Muted feminine moans echoed James's deep-throated groans.

"Damn," James swore, lifting his head abruptly. He drew in a draft of air as he stiffened his body against Isis's entrancing femininity. "If you had a middle name, it would be Circe." He stared into Isis's dark eyes while he unclasped her hands from his shoulders. Pain tore at him at the confused bewilderment he saw reflected in the luminescent pools. Damn his conscience. Damn Nora and her quest.

"I've got to go," he rasped, mentally wincing at the harsh sound of his own voice.

Isis let him step away from her once again. How many times had she obeyed her instincts and let him go while she ached with her need of him? How many more times would she have to dredge up the strength to do the same thing again? Would the promised Monday bring the answers she must have to the struggle James waged? She had to believe it would or everything that had gone before would be for nothing.

She closed her eyes to shut out the sight of him walking away. Four more days, she reminded herself as she listened for the sound of his car leaving. She would wait four more days. Then she would get her answers or know the reason why.

James was having no better success with the Monday deadline than she was. "Four days," he muttered as he entered his hotel room. He stopped before the bedroom door, his gaze focusing on the unmade bed he and Isis had so recently shared. Her scent still lingered in the air to surround him with haunting mystery. The woman was so deep inside him that her absence made him feel as if he were missing a part of his body. He had a job to do and all he could think of was having her pliant and yielding in his arms. Frustration darkened his expression as he strode irritably back toward the small bar in the sitting room. He glared at the phone on his way by. Why did Nora have to be so stubborn? If only she would release him from his promise of silence, then he could be honest with Isis. Then he could take her in truth, not this subterfuge of half-lies.

He took a mouthful of Scotch, savoring the freedom of coming to her without restraint. The highly erotic and definitely pleasurable vision burned into his mind. He groaned, involuntarily swallowing his drink at the same time. The resulting coughing fit did little to soothe his temper or his frustrated libido.

"Damn this mess," he choked roughly to the empty room. "Even when you're ten miles away, woman, you still affect me too much for my own safety."

He finished the last of the liquid more carefully, absently cradling the tumbler. He rolled it between his palms while he stared out the window. The white landscape was postcard-perfect in the silver wash of the almost full moon. Serene, calm, the scene held so many hidden dangers a man could be forgiven for succumbing to the allure of its silent beauty. His Isis was like that.

Startled at the possessive, James repeated the phrase once more. "My Isis." When had she become his, he wondered, barely aware of his temper draining away. He leaned back wearily in his chair.

Almost one whole week, he thought incredulously. I've only known her a few short days and yet I feel like a man in the middle of his first love affair. Love...? Love.

"You're mine," he promised his unseen lover and love. Soon he would hurt her. He had no choice; he was committed. But he would make it right for them again if he had to spend his whole life pursuing her. She was his just as he was hers. They belonged together, and he intended to see that Isis knew and accepted that fact.

All the pent-up energy he had been unable to release in passion was now channeled toward achieving the most important goal he had ever aimed for in his life. Failure would render every other success in ashes on his tongue. A crooked smile lifted the corner of his lips before glittering with reckless boldness in the changing depths of his eyes. He would win.

"You may want my heart skewered on a spit before this is all over, my love, but we will survive this." He nodded once before pushing himself out of his chair. "I hope you believe in marriage, because we are going to roam the world and grow old together."

Somehow with his words the room was no longer empty. Isis might have been miles away but it hardly mattered. Soon she would be permanently in his bed. He shed his clothes, then slid naked into the hollow where they had lain together. He tucked the pillow she had used against his side. It was a poor substitute, but at the moment it was all he had.

He laid an arm over the plump softness, a grin flashing in the darkness. It was a good thing no one else could see him cuddling up to a pillow. No one would believe it.

James awoke early, stretching lazily. A glance at his travel alarm confirmed the young hour. His lips twisted ruefully on his sudden realization that he and Isis had a number of minor conflicting habits to reconcile. One of them was when they slept and got up. He was a day person and she was a night. Just one more ingredient to add a little spice to their union.

Shrugging away the errant problem, James rose, showered, dressed, then sat down beside the phone.

After a quick call to room service to order a pot of hot coffee, he contacted his secretary to check in. When the coffee arrived, he poured himself a cup, then dialed his client, Nora Harris. A cultured female voice answered on the third ring.

"Have you talked to Buffy?" Nora demanded eagerly, barely giving him an opportunity to identify himself.

"Not yet. Isis and I are going to their estate this afternoon," he explained impatiently. "Once I'm inside, I'll make sure the necklace is actually there. It won't do anything for your cause if we accuse them of possessing it and then find out neither of them have it."

"Don't remind me," the older woman muttered worriedly. "You know how much I want to effect this reconciliation."

"It will work out," he reassured her.

The sigh of relief he heard brought a faint smile to his lips and an instant picture of his friend. Seemingly ageless, Nora was the polished image of sophistication and elegance. Yet, despite her wealth and social standing, she was a very real, very human lady.

"Nora." He paused, deciding to make one last attempt to persuade Nora to let him confide in Isis. He had already tried once two nights ago and failed. "I want to tell Isis. I think she can help us on this. If I run into a problem, I may need her," he explained, reaching for any reason he could think of to achieve his objective.

"No," Nora protested instantly, panic filling her voice. "Three generations of feuding families ride on this. Buffy and I must settle everything for our children's sake if not our own. I must right this before it's too late."

James knew Nora's fears, and if anyone else but Isis had been involved, he would even have agreed her reservations were well grounded. "You're mistaken if you believe she would refuse to help if she knew the whole story," he stated with firm conviction. "I've never met anyone as giving as she is. It isn't in her to refuse aid when she's needed."

"Please, James," Nora pleaded, hearing but refusing to respond to his reasoning. "Maybe I'm being too cautious. I don't know. But I do know what's at stake and I just won't risk it." She sighed softly. "If it were anything else, I'd trust your judgment."

James shook his head over her continued refusal to listen, knowing there was little he could do or say that would alter her position. "All right," he agreed finally.

"Don't be angry with me. I can tell you care about this woman—" she began.

"I love her," he corrected swiftly. "And when this tangled scheme is straightened out, I intend to marry her if she'll have me."

Nora inhaled a gasp of surprise at his unexpected words. "No wonder you want to tell her," she murmured.

"That's part of it," he admitted bluntly. "But more importantly, Isis is helping us. She deserves to know why and how she's involved." He sighed, aware that they were only going around in circles. Nora had her opinion and he had his.

"I've got to go soon. I'm picking Isis up at her place, so let me explain what I want you and Bill to do." He paused to allow her to speak. When she made no comment, he continued. "Get a flight out of New York sometime Saturday. I've reserved a suite at the Midnight Star for you. As soon as I know for sure the

Shower is there, I'll talk to Burt. He's our best bet initially. If he's receptive, I'll call you with a meeting time."

"But how are we going to get into the estate? I'm sure Buffy won't agree to see me. She hasn't in the past," Nora pointed out worriedly.

"I'm hoping that when I confront Burt with my knowledge of his possession of a necklace he knows must be stolen, he'll try to arrange a meeting between you and his wife. I'm counting on his soft spot where she's concerned, and his own dislike of publicity if it should get out that he purchased a hot necklace."

"What we're doing sounds so horrible when you put it like that," she murmured sadly. "Is it so terrible for me to right this old wrong? Buffy wants no part of me. Her refusal to listen is forcing you to lie to a woman you love and forcing me to involve you in a plan so risky I'm scared. If only grandfather had known what trouble his actions would cause."

"Don't worry," James interrupted the moment Nora took a breath. "Just bring Bill, yourself and the Blue Cascade. We've come too far to fail now."

"But Isis?"

"You leave Isis to me," he commanded sternly. "I'll work it out." He waited, stifling his impatience. He knew Nora wasn't normally an indecisive woman. But the anxiety over the family estrangement, coupled with her increasing fragility, had robbed her of her usual clear-sightedness.

"I'm being silly," she confessed shakily.

"A little," he agreed with a long-standing friend's honesty. "Just be on that plane and leave everything else to me."

James hung up a moment later, his face set in a frown. It all came down to this weekend. He had so much to do in so little time. And through it all he wanted to help Nora and still protect Isis from finding out the truth in a way too stark for her to accept or forgive. He had hoped Nora's permission to confide in her would have softened the blow. But now even that was denied him.

He paced restlessly to the window, already feeling the pain his presence would cause her. His lovemaking would look to her like a method to keep her sweet. Every word, every gesture no matter how deeply meant would be circumspect, and there wasn't a damned thing he could do about it. He raked his hand through his hair as he turned away from the mountain view he hadn't noticed. His gaze focused on his open but packed suitcase on the rack at the foot of his bed, then on the clock. Not much time before he was due to pick up Isis, he thought fatalistically as he reached for his sheared sheepskin jacket. He snapped the locks on his luggage, collected the two cases and headed for the door. Three more days to go.

"Is that all you're going to eat?" Josie demanded sternly, her hands on her hips.

Isis looked up from the article she was reading, her lips twitching with amusement at her caretaker's long-suffering tone. "It is," she agreed, giving her toasted bran muffin, decaffeinated coffee and strawberries and cream a cursory glance. "James will be here soon and I don't want to keep him waiting."

Josie sniffed disparagingly while the twinkle in her knowing eyes did nothing to strengthen her supposed ill humor. "I've a good mind to put a flea in his ear about rushing you around," she warned. "He should have stopped you from taking on this weekend," she added for good measure on seeing Isis's attention wander back to the newspaper she held.

Isis lifted her head sharply, the good mood she had awakened in dimming slightly. "What exactly does that mean?" she asked slowly, alert to the tiniest change in Josie's expression.

"What could I mean?" the older woman questioned in turn.

Isis discounted the bland innocence of her friend's reply almost instantly. Over the past few days James, Josie and Ned had become more than just friends, a fact that had surprised and pleased her. James had fit right in almost from the very start, easily charming the more talkative Josie while gaining the respect of her frequently reserved mate. Yet not once had either of them hinted at or pried into James's role in Isis's life. Until now.

"Out with it," she commanded finally, her tone gentle in spite of the inescapable demand in her words.

Josie shifted awkwardly, her lashes dropping in what was for her unusual embarrassment. Completely abandoning the original discussion, she opted for the issue bothering her. "Ned and I, we've seen the way he is with you." She paused to cast a quick glance at her employer. "More importantly, we've seen the way you are around him." She sighed gustily at Isis's unreadable expression before sinking into the chair across from her. "I don't understand why you two aren't together. Ned and I wondered if maybe it was because of us...." Her voice trailed away, leaving a hint of her unhappiness at the possibility.

"How could you be a problem?" Isis asked blankly.

"Five years ago when you offered my Ned a place with you, it was like a pot of gold at the end of the rainbow for us. With only a night watchman's job at that club and his social security, we were just barely making it. Everything we had was gone just to pay Ned's medical bills. Then you came into our lives." She silenced Isis with a gesture when she started to interrupt. "You had no family left and we had no children. It was so easy to mother you and you let us do it." She smiled slightly. "Even when you didn't need it. I like your James and so does Ned, and neither of us are so straitlaced that we can't see how attracted you two are to each other. So the only thing we could come up with was that you hadn't asked him to stay out of consideration for us." She studied Isis worriedly.

Isis met her eyes with unblinking directness. "It's not you," she answered honestly. "It's—"

"Anybody home?" James strolled through the door, a crooked grin curving his mouth. "Ned said I could come on in," he added as he came toward them. His gaze shifted from one serious face to the other. He frowned at the scene, his carefully constructed mood fading. "I'm interrupting—"

"No, no, you aren't," Josie protested, rising swiftly to her feet. "We just finished anyway." She gestured to the chair she had just vacated. "Sit down and I'll get you a cup of coffee." The last few words were tossed over her shoulder as she left the room.

"Isis?" James questioned, taking the offered place.

She shrugged, evading his curiosity. "Just a small household matter." She dipped a plump strawberry in the fresh whipped cream and lifted it to her lips for a bite, wondering at the lie she had just told. How quickly it had slipped out, almost as though she had been prepared to hide. But from what?

James stared at her, knowing how she prided herself on honesty, yet unable to accept the reason she had given him. Could she have found out why he had sought her out? Did she suspect his motives somehow? The urge to demand an answer was strong, yet he didn't dare. What if his worries were groundless?

"Want one?" Isis held another berry poised over the white fluff-filled bowl. It was a diversion but she needed to break the silence between them.

With difficulty he dragged his thoughts in order and focused on the woman he loved. "Or two, or three," he murmured, filling his mind with her. His need to store every memory, no matter how trivial, was more potent than even the fear of detection that haunted his footsteps. If, in the end, he could not keep her, then at least he would have these moments to remember.

Isis stilled, caught in the intensity of his visual hold. How could a man's eyes convey so much, the slumbering green of passion, the rich brown of strength and the golden amber of which dreams were made. No matter how many times she studied this man, there was always something new to discover about him.

He reached out to cover her fingers with his as he carried the strawberry deep into the frothy cream. Unnoticed by either of them, Josie returned with his coffee, then departed without a word.

"I've got a sweet tooth," he rasped huskily.

"So have I," Isis whispered. She lifted the now snow-covered berry. The fruit was halfway between them, a luscious, ripe and sinfully rich treat.

James leaned forward to lick the cream from his side of the strawberry. Isis was mesmerized by the eroticism of his actions. The desire in his eyes further heightened the sensuality of his gesture as he carefully ate from her hand, then slowly cleaned each of her white-tipped fingers.

"Another?" he asked with gentle roughness.

Isis inhaled sharply at his invitation. With the needs he had created in her, she would lose whatever control she had left if they stayed there one more moment. "No," she managed in a breathy purr, conveying her regret and her arousal.

James nibbled at the ends of her fingers, his gaze absorbing the exotic beauty of her features. "You're probably right," he agreed almost absently. If he lived to be a hundred, he'd never get enough of this woman. Physically and mentally she was everything he could hope for in a mate. And so responsive to his slightest touch, just as he was to her smallest gesture. She wrecked his composure more easily and far more swiftly than anyone had ever done. "We're going to be late," Isis warned, barely aware of what she was saying.

He nodded, drew back without releasing her hand and rose to his feet, drawing her with him. Josie came through the door, quietly for her, just as Isis reached his side. Still holding hands, they both turned to say goodbye to the older woman.

"You drive carefully," she directed, giving James an admonitory look. At his amused agreement she fixed Isis with a knowing stare that noted the handclasp. She nodded, then sighed gustily. "Ned was right. I had no need to worry."

That brought Isis out of the sensual fog that surrounded her. She eyed her friend, silently demanding she refrain from her usual outspoken candor. "Ned usually is," she pointed out dryly, before giving James a smile. She studiously ignored his curious scrutiny as she headed for the door with him right beside her. "My car or yours?"

He paused in the foyer to shrug into his jacket after helping Isis with hers.

She glanced at him through her lashes just in time to catch his unconcerned shrug. Only moments before he had been as affected by her as she was by him. Yet now his desire was gone, replaced by the possessive caring he had shown her from the first. She could have felt deprived, but strangely she didn't. She knew a touch of her hand, a certain look would reignite the flame that burned in him. It was heady knowledge, both powerful and humbling.

"Yours will be fine." He tucked her hand in his pocket before opening the door, and ushered her outside and down the path to her Trans-Am.

"How did you know?" she demanded when she had settled behind the wheel. His suitcase lay on the seat behind hers where he had obviously put it before he came in.

James grinned at her amazed tone. "Maybe your mind-reading abilities are rubbing off on me," he teased, buckling himself into the passenger seat. He chuckled at her skeptical look. "Actually, Ned told me he had loaded your clothes in this car without asking you."

Her lips twisted wryly. "I can see I'm getting too predictable. It's unnerving how he and Josie anticipate my needs."

"Which brings me to the question I've been wanting to ask. What was Ned right about?"

Ten

Isis's fingers tightened on the wheel at the unexpected question. Remembering her lie, her mind went unforgivably blank. She could feel James staring at her as she automatically guided her car down the twisting road.

"It was about you, actually," she admitted finally, seeing no other way to answer him.

"And?" he probed, watching her closely.

Isis flicked him a quick look before deciding to be honest. She would rather confess her first falsehood than continue deceiving him. "Josie had been wondering if she and Ned were intruding. Ned tried to tell her they weren't. She didn't believe him."

James's brow rose at the swift succession of precise sentences. His gaze roamed briefly over her deep gold fur jacket to the cinnamon jeans tucked into matching fur boots. He wondered at the tension visible in every line of her body.

"You might as well know I lied earlier when you asked me what Josie and I were talking about," she added when he remained silent. "We were discussing—"

"Why I haven't stayed with you," he finished for her, suddenly understanding.

He should have known. He would have to be blind and stupid not to know how confused Isis was by his insistence on bringing her home every evening and never staying overnight at her house. Sometimes he wasn't sure he understood himself. He just knew he couldn't let her make a real place for him in her life until she knew everything.

Isis said nothing. After all, what was there left to say? She and James had come together in passion, had shared thoughts, more hers than his, yet so much was still hidden. He had promised to reveal himself on Monday, and she waited because she loved him. She was doing her best to ignore her uncertainty, her curiosity and the hurt his secret caused her. But it was difficult, so very difficult.

"Tell me what you know about Burt Metcalf and his wife," James suggested, latching on to the first diversion that came to mind. Anything was preferable to the silence between them. He couldn't afford to dwell on Isis's feelings at this moment. If he did, he might break Nora's confidence, and his own code, and tell her everything.

Isis seized the abrupt change of topic gratefully. "I met them in Atlantic City earlier in the tour," she explained after a short pause. "They came back to my dressing room after my first show and were in the audience every night until I closed."

"It's the wife, Buffy, who's interested in the psychic world, isn't it?" James prompted.

Isis nodded before giving him a swift, curious glance. "Yes, but Burt is becoming very intrigued himself. He's quite devoted to Buffy, so I think that's part of the attraction."

"What are your plans for this weekend? Will you be doing anything special?"

Isis negotiated a particularly sharp curve while considering her answer. "Not really. I think I'll just wait and see how things go. I know Buffy would like to know about my background...how I realized I was psychic, how I developed my skills." She shrugged lightly. "I think she wants to try her hand a bit."

Startled, James stared at her. "Is that possible?"

"Depends on what 'authority' you listen to. Personally, I've always believed each of us is capable of some form of paranormal ability. But, as with any other talent, it must be exercised and sharpened with use. You don't just decide to read minds, have precognitive dreams or whatever. Even after working to strengthen and perfect an ability, I think the level you reach depends on the individual."

She stared at the road stretching in front of her, hearing her words echo in her head. The relatively straight asphalt ribbon rolled monotonously past as James thought over what she had said.

Necklace. Where? Time short.

Isis's eyes widened as the words whispered through her mind. She shook her head, knowing they came from James. Was the necklace the Sapphire Shower he had told her about? And if it was, why was he wondering where? What time was short? This weekend? Their time together? Or some other time she knew nothing about?

"What are you intending to do this weekend?" she asked. She refused to attempt to read his thoughts although she had no qualms about questioning him. This glimpse had been accidental and therefore forgivable.

James tensed, eyeing her warily. Being around her held an element of risk. At any moment she could turn her power on him. Even though she understated her accuracy, he doubted she would miss anything. "I thought I'd get to know Metcalf a little better before I approached him," he admitted cautiously.

Isis considered his plan, a faint frown marring her brow. "Now that I think about it, that seems like a roundabout approach for a straightforward business deal."

He heard the suspicion in her voice and silently berated himself for having forgotten to guard his thoughts. She had warned him that intense concentration by anyone near her usually intruded whether she meant it to or not. "With a reclusive man like Metcalf, sometimes it's the only way," he parried with studied indifference. "Remember, I'm the one seeking to buy. He's not hunting for a purchaser. It's up to me to woo him."

"Perhaps," she conceded, tacitly admitting her lack of knowledge in his arena. Yet despite his reasonable answers, she still was more uneasy than ever. So many questions, so many logical responses that fit, yet not quite. Her body and her heart had trusted him in passion and in love. Yet she had questions, so many questions.

Conversation was sporadic for the rest of the trip. Although James tried to recapture the easy intimacy of earlier drives, Isis found herself holding back. She wanted to eliminate the alienated feeling plaguing her, yet no matter how hard she tried, she couldn't.

There was a storm on the horizon. She could see it in her mind's eye as clearly as she traced the cloudless cerulean sky overhead. Tension, like summer lightning, shimmered around her. If she reached out her hand she could touch James, her lover, yet not her mate. Some part of him was withdrawing from her with every mile closer they came to the Metcalf estate.

When she guided the sleek jet-black car through the scrolled metal gates guarding the grounds, she glanced at his face. The unreadable mask she saw told its own story. "We're here," she murmured unnecessarily.

He turned to her, his lips lifting in a parody of his usual crooked grin. "So we are." He gestured toward the house just as she pulled to a stop in front of the wide stone steps. "I guess it's time for us both to go to work."

Isis stared at him, hearing the gravity beneath his teasing words. The serious tone mirrored the determined gleam in his eyes. Neither matched his careful banter.

"As you say," she agreed at length, taking shelter behind the screen of her lashes to hide her disappointment.

With her face turned away she reached for the handle of her door. His hand closed over hers, stilling her movements.

"Isis, I—" he began.

She swiftly cut through his hesitant opening. "No more, James. Not unless today is Monday." She pulled her fingers out of his warm grasp, immediately aware of the chill of separation. Part of her cried out at the loss. She wanted nothing more than to swing around and find herself in his arms, but she didn't even look at him.

She couldn't, not right now. Instead, she stared at the two-story building before her.

"Something's going to happen here," she whispered, following the script written in her mind. She shuddered as the cold wind of a future yet unveiled drifted over her. "Long years of pain—you have come." She inhaled deeply as the fleeting message disappeared. The scene righted itself and once again she was back in the car with James at her side.

She turned her head slowly, drawn against her will to look at him. He was pale beneath his tan, his unguarded gaze reflecting a rainbow of emotions. "You knew about me before you came, didn't you?" It was a statement, not a question. Isis saw him register her certainty. She caught a glimpse of the lie he started to tell. Her brow rose, daring him to utter the falsehood.

"I did," he responded finally, his voice flat with its lack of emotion. "I needed to get here in the shortest possible time. You were the only way I could do it. I needed you then. I still need you now." He waited, tension coiling in his stomach at her probing assessment. He felt perspiration drip down his back as she sat as unmoving as the mountains in the distance.

"You offer me no answer still."

"I can't."

She glanced briefly toward the entrance of the main house. The front door was opening. In seconds they would greet their hosts. She refocused on James, concentrating on his thoughts. His lie had given her the right to utilize her skill. "I will ask one question. I want a truthful answer. If you lie, we leave." She waited for his nod of understanding before continuing. "Whatever you do here, is it dishonest—legally dishonest?"

James met her eyes, relief coursing through him at her demand. "It is not," he responded simply. He lifted his hand to touch her cheek, but she drew back, her eyes almost black with the restraint she placed on her emotions. He let his arm drop to his side, his lips twisting ruefully. "In spite of what it looks like, I've never deliberately lied to you. Held things back, yes, but not lied."

It was a plea, the only one he could make. He searched her face for some small sign of her generosity or understanding. There was none. Her exotic features held all the mystery of the ancient Sphinx. The car door opened with a click as she slid out without a word.

He sighed wearily as he got out, feeling more defeated than he had ever felt in his life. She would help him but that was all. Whatever had gone before was done. Her pain and disappointment when he had admitted the truth had been agonizingly obvious. Now no expression remained in her eyes, only chilling blankness. She had closed herself off from him. He was never more sure of that than when they stood facing each other in the spacious bedroom suite the Metcalfs had allotted them.

"I don't suppose you have a solution?" Isis queried, sinking with fluid grace onto the hunter-green velvet chaise by the window. "There's one bed and two of us."

He glared at the disputed furniture, wondering why he hadn't foreseen such an obvious development. After all, in Isis's business, "bringing a friend" meant arriving with a sleeping partner. "You're as safe as you want to be," he bit out, swinging around to confront her. "You were no unwilling partner before, and you won't be now." He lifted his hand in a wide sweeping arc to encompass their plush surroundings. "It doesn't matter to me whether we have one room or ten. I won't lay a finger on you if that's what you want."

Isis drew herself up, suddenly angry at the way he had phrased his assurance.

James caught her look and matched it with one of his own. "Damn it, woman, I did everything I could to stay out of your bed." He raked his fingers through his hair, frustrated with the whole situation. Aggravated annoyance marked his face with deep, tense lines.

"I'll vouch for that," Isis agreed acidly before she thought.

James stared at her in silence, his eyes glittering with temper. The unflinching way she faced him held a regal dignity he had to admire. Gradually his anger died, leaving him with only one clear fact. He loved this woman. He had to make her see how much he regretted this role he had been forced to play, and yelling at her was no way to accomplish that. As it was he didn't have much time because the Metcalfs were waiting for them downstairs.

"Will you listen to me for a second?" he asked quietly as he sat down on the edge of the bed. He would rather have shared her chaise but he doubted she was ready to allow that.

Isis searched his face, seeing the determination etched there. Not now, she begged silently. She had to stay angry; it was the only defense she had against the reality of his betrayal. Yet even as she tried to hold on to her emotional shield, it slipped away at his pleading, almost desperate appeal. She fought to ignore the pain she saw in him. It was a losing battle. Her heart simply refused to accept the dictates of her mind.

"All right," she agreed tonelessly.

"I love you, Isis." The words rushed from his mouth in an explosion of urgency over which he had no control. He gazed into her startled eyes. "I admit I sought you out, but I'm asking you to trust me. There are reasons I can't explain for everything I've done."

"You've said all that before. Nothing's really changed," she interrupted swiftly, unable to stand hearing any more of his vague promises. If he loved her, he would trust her enough to confide in her.

He was waiting, watching her with those expressive eyes of his. She refused to see the love shining there, the passion her body remembered all too well. To see was to admit how important he had become to her.

"It doesn't matter to you that I love you, does it?" he demanded, his voice husky with feeling.

"How can it? To love is to trust," she countered woodenly. "You ask for my trust, yet you offer me none. What's this secret you guard so jealously? Who do you protect? Another woman?" Her expression tightened at his betraying flinch when her shot in the dark went home. She surged to her feet, her hands clenching into fists at the feminine outrage firing her blood.

James got up to move swiftly to her side. "It's not what you're thinking," he tried to explain, reaching out to catch her shoulders.

The moment Isis felt his touch, she whirled on him, her eyes twin flames of sapphire wrath. "For once in my life, I wish I were a man," she lashed out, her anger spilling over in a tumble of hot words.

James grabbed her arms, being careful in his temper of her satiny skin. "Stop it," he commanded roughly. "You are my only lover. There is no other woman I want or need but you." He shook her once, demanding her attention. "Believe that, Isis, for both our sakes."

Isis struggled in his hold, vainly trying to free herself. Finally, when no amount of wiggling gained her the space she needed, she allowed her head to fall back so that she was staring into his eyes. They were alive with emotion. They sizzled, they burned, they held her in an unbreakable snare. There was a fierce tension in his body. She felt it with every quick breath she drew. The heat of him surrounded her, scenting the air with his pure male fragrance. Memories of their shared passion, their desire rose in her mind like unwanted ghosts.

"Damn you, James. I loved you. I trusted you even when I knew you were hiding something," she whispered, as her eyes filled with tears. Her voice was a bitter shell that just escaped a sob. She was drained of all feeling, too weary to fight him.

"Don't," James groaned, drawing her unresisting body against him. He cradled her against his strength, trying to absorb the shudders rippling through her delicately fashioned frame. He stroked her back, smoothing the wool crepe blouse she wore over her skin as he gentled her with his voice.

Isis pressed her face into his shoulder, drawing comfort from the almost sexless way he held her. His whispered words soothed the trembling of her limbs as she rested against him. When he swept her into his arms, she made no protest. She was beyond caring at that moment. Her mind was blank of all thought, all emotion.

James laid her carefully on the bed and pulled off her fur boots. Then he drew the pale green comforter lying folded across the footboard over her. He brushed the tangled curls of her face with a light hand.

"Sleep, my love. Forget for now what you think I've done and rest. I'll make your excuses to our hosts."

Isis gazed at him, mesmerized by the tenderness of his tone as he sat beside her. The hypnotic stroking of her hair was pleasantly soothing. Her lashes drooped wearily. She should get up, she told herself, but somehow she just couldn't make her muscles obey her orders. The cushiony softness of the bed, coupled with the lightweight warmth of the down coverlet, seemed to draw what little strength she had left. Everything was gone. Her anger, her strength of will and body. A strange lassitude descended, her breathing slowed until finally she drifted off.

James lifted his hand away, his eyes never leaving her face. In response her faintly foreign features were even more breathtaking in their stark simplicity. His jaw clenched as a diamond tear slipped through the dam of her ebony lashes to trickle down her cheek. He put out a finger to catch the crystalline droplet. He stared at the moisture on the tip for a moment before carrying it to his lips.

How bitter it tasted. Her pain was his if she but knew it. He closed his eyes against the sight of her. What if he could never make this right? He shook his head, forcing the traitorous thought aside. He had to. She was his. He wanted no other woman in his life.

With a weary sigh he rose and headed for the door without a backward look. He opened it, stopped short, almost colliding with his hostess.

"Isn't Isis coming down?" Buffy Metcalf asked with barely disguised eagerness.

He stepped into the corridor, easing the door shut behind him. "A little later," he explained casually. "She's resting now."

Buffy's carefully made-up face mirrored her disappointment. "I should have thought of that." She smiled hesitantly. "Burt told me how exhausting this last tour has been, but I so wanted to talk to her."

James made himself smile at the older woman he had come to meet. In a way it was easy to like her. She was so like Nora it was uncanny.

"Yes, it was very tiring," he agreed as they walked slowly down the open hall to the stairs. "Isis's ability requires a great deal of concentration, as you probably know."

Buffy nodded, her artistically arranged silver curls shimmering gently with the gesture. "Have you known her long?" she asked. She touched his arm lightly, her pale blue eyes a mixture of curiosity and friendliness.

"A while," he murmured vaguely, softening his reply with a more natural grin. Buffy was a much easier person to like than the reports had led him to believe. In spite of the sleek luxury of her home, the tasteful but hardly discreet jewels decorating her throat and ears, and the designer clothes, she was as artless as a child.

"Tell me, do you work with Isis?" She peered up at him through mascaraed lashes.

"No, as a matter of fact, I handle jewelry and precious gems," he replied easily. He stopped on the next-to-last step to run his eyes appreciatively over the gems she wore. "Those are lovely pieces."

Buffy preened visibly. "Did you hear that, Burt? James likes my diamonds."

James glanced around to find his host walking across the entrance hall toward them.

Burt gazed at his petite wife indulgently. "You haven't been showing off again, have you, honey?" he queried as he slipped his arm around her shoulders.

Buffy pouted playfully. "I haven't. James just was telling me he's in the jewelry business."

Burt's shrewd eyes held interest as he looked him over. "Are you now?" he murmured, his tone noncommittal.

James inclined his head, slipping into his blend-into-the-scenery role. "Only in a minor way," he confessed with the proper amount of diffidence. Burt Metcalf was no fool. Until he was certain the Sapphire Shower was on the premises, he didn't dare make a move to confront his host, nor to plead Nora's cause.

Oblivious to the assessment taking place between the two men, Buffy laid her hand on her husband's arm. "Let's go into the lounge. Soames should have refreshments waiting for us by now."

James glanced down at the woman at his side, quickly following her lead. He knew without looking that Burt had put his own interpretation on his slightly less than polished behavior. It was an evaluation he took pains to foster during the long get-acquainted conversation that followed. No mention was made of gems again, yet he was satisfied with his progress so far. Now, if he could just locate the Sapphire Shower.

Eleven

——————

Isis awoke slowly, drifting reluctantly up from the depths of sleep. She opened her eyes to the darkened room, knowing she was alone. She should get up, shower and dress, but at the moment she just didn't want to make the effort. The longer she could put off facing James and making polite conversation, the better.

"James," she sighed sadly as the full spectrum of her memory flooded her. Two days to see him, to talk to him, to pretend there was no rift between them. Two nights to share this room, possibly this bed— The door clicked open quietly, interrupting her thoughts. Her eyes widened at the silhouette poised on the threshold. The light from the hall outlined James's form all too clearly. Despite her hurt, her sense of betrayal, Isis was aware of the attraction he still had for her. Suddenly the darkness was less cold and empty, more warm and welcoming. Biting her lip against her body's traitorous responses, she watched him shut the door, sealing the room once more in velvet shadows. She felt rather than saw him approach the bed. The mattress dipped ever so gently beneath his carefully lowered weight. The sound of his breathing mingled with hers in the silence.

"Are you feeling better?" he asked quietly, making no effort to touch her.

Isis started slightly at his question, a faint gasp escaping her lips. He must have cat's eyes to see in the dark, she thought inconsequentially. "Yes," she replied briefly.

He sighed before reaching out to touch her face. "Are you still angry?" He lightly traced the exquisitely molded curve of her cheek, his gaze riveted on the pale silver shadows cast on her skin by the moonlight from the open window.

"Don't," she pleaded, feeling the heat of desire fanning to life. She wouldn't give in to his appeal. She would be strong.

"Don't pleasure you?" he countered, his voice rich with tenderness and the deep, dark memories of their passion. "Your skin's like velvet, goddess. I want to stroke you, hold you next to my heart, feel you explode with wanting me in my arms."

Isis lifted her hand to catch his tormenting fingers. "You're not playing fair."

"I'm not playing anything," he denied immediately.

Isis put his hand from her before pushing herself into a sitting position. There was an unwanted intimacy in lying in bed with James sitting beside her and only the moon for a light. She had to make him understand her dilemma. Her emotions were too raw to handle him and their close quarters.

"You've got to leave me alone. We're here. I've given my word to do this weekend with you for whatever reasons you have. We're stuck in this room for the next two nights and two days. I won't spend my time fighting your attempts at seduction."

James leaned forward to switch on the bedside lamp. They both blinked to adjust to the sudden intrusion of the soft illumination. "Seduction?" he demanded after a short pause. He stared at her intently, one brow quirking upward to indicate his dislike of her description. "I've never seduced you and I'm not about to start now. You're too strong a woman for any man to demand and get submission. You were with me all the way." He covered her lips with his fingers when she would have interrupted. "That's a compliment, my love," he added, eyeing her militant expression perceptively.

Isis's temper drove the remaining lethargy from her body. Compliment? By whose standards? "My love?" she repeated, glaring at him the moment he removed his hand. "I'm not your anything and I'll thank you to remember that."

James shook his head, his lips twitching at her irritation. He should be ashamed of himself for provoking her but the life flowing back into her was too rewarding. Her cheeks held more than a hint of color and her eyes fairly spit sparks at him. The drawn, pale look and the lackluster eyes of earlier were gone. She was fighting with him. And that, even at the risk of any number of verbal scratch marks, was preferable to her hurting.

"How about if I named you my wife?" he asked, cocking his head to one side. He just barely managed to stifle a grin at her incensed outrage. If it had been humanly possible, there would have been steam coming out of her ears.

Isis tossed her head, the tumble of ebony hair dancing with primitive abandon about her shoulders. "You're crazy," she bit out, throwing back the coverlet with one quick jerk. "Would you mind?" She frowned at him when he made no effort to get up so she could get out of bed. It galled her to ask him for anything, but she would be darned if she'd bounce ignominiously across the king-size mattress to the other side.

"Certainly," he responded, rising slowly to his feet. "I guess it is time we changed for dinner." He turned away, pulling his shirt out of his pants as he did so.

Isis stood up, momentarily taken aback at his calm acceptance of her rejection. Her eyes narrowed as his shirt was flipped across the room to land half on and half off the chair by the chaise longue.

"You're not undressing in here, are you?" she snapped, her gaze focused on the golden skin rippling gracefully over his muscled back. Blast him. Why couldn't there be some blemish on him? Why did she have to remember the feel of him against her so well?

James glanced over a bare shoulder, his face a picture of innocent inquiry. "Where would you like me to undress?"

Isis forced her eyes to lift to his. Remember, he lied, she reminded herself. He used you to help another woman. "In the bathroom," she managed, trying to ignore the devilish gleam in his eyes. He knew she had been watching him, darn him.

He shrugged lightly, a move too subtle to be a blatant play for her attention even if he did get it anyway.

"If you like, but I had an idea you might want the shower first."

Isis jammed her fists on her hips, her sock-covered toes beating an annoyed rhythm on the imported rug. "I would," she decided finally. She padded past him to the closet, vaguely aware that sometime during her nap someone had come in and unpacked. She hurriedly sorted through her clothes for a robe. With a deft flick of her wrist, she pulled the peacock-decorated silk from the hanger, tossed it over one shoulder and stalked into the bathroom. She all but slammed the door shut before loudly clicking the lock. The muffled masculine chuckle from the bedroom made her grit her teeth angrily.

"Obnoxious, insensitive, deceitful liar," she mumbled, turning on the shower full blast. She undressed with more speed than grace before stepping into the jade-tiled stall. "If you stay this aggravating the whole weekend, I won't have the least trouble resisting your manly charms, James Leland."

She worked up a vigorous lather, washed, rinsed and dried to the tune of indistinct mumblings. The fact that she was acting out of character bothered her not one whit. Somehow James always seemed to bring out the worst in her. Or the best, a little voice inside her head whispered.

Isis thrust her bare arms into the robe before wrapping it around her shower-fresh body and securing the gold tassel tie. She would not remember how James had brought out her best. She would remember how he tricked her into bringing him here. She pulled open the door, almost cannoning into him. Carefully, she unplastered her nose from his chest and glared at him. She would not succumb to his appeal, and she darned well would not notice how his voice seemed to stroke her senses with velvet.

He grinned while he eyed her with bold appreciation. "That was fast." His stance, in fact everything about him, challenged her to do her worst and then forgive him.

She sidestepped him, holding on to her temper. He wasn't going to succeed in getting around her. "It won't work."

One brow lifted as his gaze followed her to the closet. "What won't?" he asked, making no attempt to disguise his humor.

Isis refused to so much as look over her shoulder. "I'm too tired for these games. You got what you wanted. I was dumb enough to fall for your helpless act once. I won't be again." She reached for the long, black silk dress embossed with silver medallions that she planned to wear. "The sooner this weekend's over, the better." She walked across to the chaise and draped her selection over one end.

James watched her unconsciously graceful movements for a second before he spoke. "Believe me, you don't want this over with one bit more than I do," he added, his tone deep with conviction.

Caught by the gravity in his words, Isis swung around, only to find him disappearing into the bathroom. He closed the door with a soft click before she could say anything. She stood staring at the blank panel. Somehow she was no longer angry. Her mood was gone almost as quickly as it had come. Once again she was aware of a bone-deep exhaustion that was a product of too little sleep, missed meals, constant demands on her physical and mental strength. And James's advent into her life. He had caught her at one of her most vulnerable times. Right now, she simply wasn't strong enough to try to make sense out of his actions and her own emotions. She needed a respite and a quiet place. She had neither.

Isis stroked her temples lightly, already feeling the strain of her soul-searching. She still had to dress and go downstairs to be polite to her hosts. Sighing at the unappealing prospect, she sat before the vanity to make up her face. As she stared at the pale reflection, she almost wished for some of her James-induced temper back. At least then she wouldn't look and feel so impossibly drained. She picked up the pot of foundation and began spreading it on with smooth, even strokes.

By the time James reentered the bedroom, Isis had completed her cosmetic ritual and styled her hair in the tumbling cascade held in place by a delicately wrought silver band. The simple arrangement was one of her favorites when she wasn't working. It was easily managed and very comfortable with its absence of pins.

"I like that gold stuff you used on your eyes," James commented, digging into a drawer for his socks.

Startled at his compliment, Isis paused, her fingers hovering over the gilded tie at her waist. "You do?" she asked, wondering at the ease with which he was padding about the bedroom in his briefs getting ready.

"Uh-huh," he grunted, glancing up as he pulled on his second sock. "Don't you think you'd better finish getting ready?" He rose and picked up the slacks he had laid out only moments before. "We don't have much time," he added.

Isis stared at him, a little taken aback at his behavior. The way he was acting, they could have been a married couple of twenty or thirty years. I like that gold stuff. Hurry up, dear, or we'll be late. He even grunted like a long-wedded husband.

Barely aware of what she was doing, Isis discarded her robe in favor of the silk off-the-shoulder dress. If he wasn't bothered about the situation between them, why should she be, she decided.

"Ready?" James questioned minutes later.

"I guess," she agreed, taking one last look in the mirror.

"Aren't you wearing any jewelry?"

She frowned at her reflection, suddenly realizing she hadn't put on her earrings. The dramatic simplicity of her gown needed little embellishment except for the long silver-and-onyx dangles she had gotten in Egypt for her seventeenth birthday. James waited patiently while she corrected her omission.

"Done," she murmured, giving her head a slight toss to be sure the pierced ornaments were securely fastened. The delicate strands dripping with ebony stones flicked against her neck, gleaming softly in the light.

"Let me." He held open the sheer matching wrap.

Isis turned around to allow him to drape it over her shoulders. At another time she would have wondered at her docility, but not tonight. Somehow James's attitude supported her without demanding anything in return. His eyes told her she was beautiful, yet his touch was light, almost casual. She had no explanation for his attitude, but she couldn't help being grateful for it. Some of the tension she was barely aware of eased. Maybe this evening and the time following would be less demanding than she'd thought.

She was silent as she walked beside him downstairs, unwilling to disturb whatever accord lay between them. He directed her across the wide stone entranceway toward a set of open double doors. She caught her breath at the panoramic view of the lake the semicircular windows provided as she entered.

"Unbelievable, isn't it?" Buffy remarked, coming toward them with a smile.

Isis focused on the petite woman in front of her. "And unexpected," she added truthfully.

Buffy gestured toward the setting of cream tweed couches facing the glass overlook. "Shall we sit down? Burt will see to your drinks. White wine, wasn't it?"

Isis nodded before following Buffy to the love seat nearest the rough stone fireplace on the far wall. "This is an unusual room."

Burt appeared at her elbow, a tulip glass in one hand and a tumbler with bourbon and water for James in the other. "One of a kind," he explained proudly, his rather heavy features lightening with a faint smile. "I never could stand having something just like someone else's. When I was younger my family had too many mouths to feed on too little money. Always swore if I hit it rich, I'd spoil myself." He nodded decisively. "I have, too."

"Now, Burt," Buffy chided, giving her husband an indulgent look. "You're making yourself sound like a despot or something."

Isis took a hasty sip of her drink in an attempt to stifle her amusement at Buffy's scolding of her spouse. Having been on the receiving end of one of the tough businessman's tirades, she was surprised to see him chastised. She felt James shift slightly in his place beside her. She risked a glance at his face to find him struggling with the same emotions she had. The corners of his lips were twitching, hinting at the control he exercised as Buffy added another admonition to the first.

"So tell me how you got started mind reading," Buffy demanded eagerly.

The abrupt subject change caught Isis off guard, startling her. The sight of her hostess perched like a bright-eyed bird on the arm of Burt's chair nearly finished what the older woman's correction of her husband had started.

She swallowed quickly and put down her glass while ignoring the silent laughter she could feel rippling through James's body. "Actually it was an accident," she began hurriedly. "You have to remember I spent my first seventeen years in a primitive culture compared to ours, and I was surrounded by a history where soothsayers and diviners were more normal than they are today. It would have been odd had I not been influenced by the things around me. Add to that a fey Irish father and there was no escaping having some psychic ability."

"Did you study to learn how to do different things?"

Isis shook her head. "No. At first it was nothing more than a game, an amusing trick if you will. I occasionally did a little act at my sorority house in college. Because of my background and my gift I became much more popular than I expected."

Buffy leaned forward, her expression alive with interest. The two men were forgotten as she explored the subject so close to her heart. "So you graduated, then went into the club routine?"

Again Isis shook her head, a tiny smile playing about her lips. "Hardly. I have a master's in library science."

"You're a librarian?" Burt voiced his disbelief, speaking for the first time.

"I am." She chuckled at the Metcalfs' duplicate expressions of skepticism. She glanced at James, remembering his similar reaction when she had first told him. The glimmer of laughter in his eyes confirmed his recall of the same incident. For a second they shared their silent amusement, unconsciously excluding the older couple.

"So how long did you work as a librarian?" James prompted.

"Six months," she replied, quickly taking her cue. "Then I started the club circuit."

"Dinner is served."

The dignified announcement fell into a pool of silence, drawing everyone's eyes to the door off to one side. A sparse-looking man stood rigidly on the threshold.

Buffy wrinkled her nose, a gesture more suited to a young girl than a mature woman. Yet the juvenile action suited her open, guileless personality perfectly. "We'll be right there, Soames." She rose with a charmingly apologetic smile. "He keeps us all so well organized. If it were left up to me, poor Burt would exist on TV dinners and take-out chicken." She giggled engagingly as she tucked her hand in the crook of her husband's arm.

Isis rose, casting James a sidelong glance beneath her lashes. The flicker of amusement in his gaze silently reinforced her own opinion of Buffy's childlike candor. Obviously he liked the older woman, too.

Dinner was a beautifully prepared meal served with all the pomp of an elaborate occasion. Buffy's naïve enjoyment, and even Burt's more sedate remarks, added a surprising degree of friendliness. The often ruthless and frequently irritable man Isis had seen so far was softened by his wife's gentling influence and the comfort of his home. By the time the four of them adjourned to the overlook and settled down with an after-dinner brandy, Burt was almost as talkative as his mate.

"Burt likes your friend very much," Buffy observed, a twinkle in her eyes.

Isis turned her head toward the two men as they stood facing each other beside the fireplace. Elbows propped on the satin-smooth wood mantel, they were discussing the merits of various sports cars.

"They do seem to have found a mutual interest," Isis agreed with a faint smile. She glanced back at her hostess. As she did so, her long earrings brushed against her neck, catching the light.

Buffy stared at the delicately wrought adornments, admiration evident in her expression. "I've been meaning to tell you all evening how much I adore your earrings. Where did you get them?"

"Cairo," Isis replied, lightly fingering one jet-and-silver ornament.

Buffy sighed theatrically. "Wouldn't you know it? I do so love jewelry. It's a mania with me." She leaned forward, lowering her voice to a conspiratorial level. "Burt just got me the most gorgeous necklace that has been in and out of my family for years." She cast a quick peek over her shoulder before continuing. "It's the most fantastic thing imaginable, but I can't wear it anywhere because it's so elaborate."

"That's a shame," Isis responded, wondering where she was leading with her confidences. So far this evening the other woman's conversation had been anything but predictable.

"Would you like to see it?" She eyed Isis expectantly. When she hesitated, Buffy's enthusiastic expression dimmed slightly. "I thought with your obvious love of clothes and jewelry you'd like to—" she began awkwardly.

"I would, very much," Isis assured her hurriedly. Just for a fleeting second she had wondered if Buffy's necklace was the same one James had come to buy. From his very cursory description, it seemed to be a possibility. If it were the piece, Buffy was definitely not interested in selling. Obviously whatever Buffy wanted, Burt would support.

"You're sure?" Buffy questioned anxiously, despite the excitement coloring her voice.

"Sure about what?" Burt asked, coming over to stand beside his wife.

Buffy gazed up at him. "I was just telling Isis about the Sapphire Shower. I thought she might enjoy seeing it."

At the mention of the Sapphire Shower, Isis lifted her eyes to James's face. He stood just to the right of Burt's left shoulder, his gaze focused on the nearly empty snifter he held. He showed no recognition of the name, nor did he appear more than politely interested when he raised his head.

Isis studied him curiously, suddenly aware of something she had noticed vaguely during the course of the evening. James was different. He was no longer the dynamic, appealing male who had been romancing her the whole week. Instead he was that fade-into-the-woodwork, nice man she had first noticed in her audience.

A faint frown pleated her brow as the sound of her name penetrated her absorption. She cleared her expression instantly to turn a smile on Buffy and her husband.

"I'm sorry. I was miles away," she apologized as she placed her empty crystal on the coffee table before her.

"I was asking if you'd like to see the Shower now?"

"Definitely," she agreed, rising to her feet. Her dress swirled gracefully about her ankles as she accepted the hand James held out to her. His fingers closed around hers in a lover's clasp. But there was nothing lovable about the warning he exerted with a brief tightening of his grip.

"I believe I've heard something about a Sapphire Shower," he remarked casually as they strolled across the hall toward another set of double doors.

Isis heard him begin his charade in silent shock. What was he up to? Why was he pretending so little interest in the very thing he had said he came to get? Surely his need for an oblique approach couldn't extend as far as this? Had she been mistaken in him? Had she seen integrity where there was none?

More questions. Again no answers. She had to know soon what he was doing and why.

Twelve

——

It's exquisite," Isis breathed. She stared at the sparkling jewels connected by a fine web of silver. Deep blue stones dropped in graduated raindrops from a matched circlet of faceted games of the same hue. "I can see how it got its name."

Buffy lifted the necklace from its bed of white velvet. "It was my grandmother's coming-of-age gift. She named it," she explained, her gaze tracing the design of the antique.

"Heirlooms always seem to mean so much more than their monetary value when they're handed down from parent to child," Isis agreed, seeing the other woman's absorbed interest. "The family history must mean a lot to you."

Buffy looked up, her expression altering visibly. The childlike aura that was so much a part of her personality was gone, leaving behind a determination and anger that was as startling as it was unexpected.

"The history of this piece is not something I want to remember. It cost my father his fortune. He lost everything, including his love for the twin brother who ruined him, just to possess the Shower." Her fingers closed around the necklace protectively. "But now it's back where it belongs. One day I will be able to give it to my daughter."

Shocked at the vehemence in Buffy's usually bubbly voice, Isis studied her a moment. If she had been sure Buffy would hold on to her treasure before, she was doubly so now. There was no way James would be able to purchase the Shower.

She turned her head slightly to stare at James, expecting to see her realization in his expression. What she saw was a faint nod, almost as though he had known about Buffy's feelings beforehand. Perplexed, Isis frowned thoughtfully as Buffy replaced the Sapphire Shower in its case.

How could he have known about Buffy's intense reaction to the jewels if he didn't know the person involved? She tipped her head, barely aware of the small conversation taking place between Buffy and Burt as they locked the Shower away in the hidden wall safe at the far side of the study. Her whole attention was centered on James.

He met her look without blinking, his expression closed to her. Nothing showed, no emotion, no telltale muscle movements, no change of any kind.

"Will ten tomorrow morning be all right with you?" Buffy asked as she and her husband rejoined them. Once more she was the vivacious creature she normally was.

Startled out of her fruitless contemplation, Isis glanced at the other woman. "That's fine," she agreed, striving to attain the properly enthusiastic role required of her. After all, the meeting was one of the main reasons she had come.

"It looks like you and I will be deserted for a couple of hours while our ladies discuss their psychic interests," Burt remarked, giving James a man-to-man look.

"So it does," he responded neutrally. Neither by word nor gesture did he betray his need for the privacy Isis's discussion would provide to talk to Burt about the Sapphire Shower.

Burt nodded, his dark eyes lighting with a controlled gleam of anticipation. "Buffy is not the only one into gems. I do a bit of collecting myself, semiprecious mostly. Would you like to take a look at them while they're busy?" he asked.

"Yes," he answered simply.

He touched Isis's arm lightly to indicate his readiness to make his good-night. Moments later he and Isis parted from the older couple in front of their door.

"Now what?" Isis demanded the second they had gained the privacy of their room.

James shrugged faintly as he released her. He forced himself to meet her eyes calmly. He had to keep a tight rein on the desire she inspired in him or he would take her in his arms and damn the consequences. "We sleep, what else?"

"You've got to be kidding," she returned swiftly, casting a significant glance over the wide bed. "I'm not sleeping with you in that." She stalked across the room to the chaise by the window. "One of us can use this."

James looked first at one piece of furniture, then the other before studying her no-nonsense stance. He wanted to remind her how often over the past few days she had wanted to sleep with him the night through. The shimmer of pain beneath the open defiance in her eyes stopped him from saying a word. In spite of the act she had put on downstairs, she was still hurting from finding out about why he had approached her. And whether she knew it or not, he was aching for both of them.

He stared across the space separating them, wishing he dared hold her. She looked as brittle as hoarfrost as she faced him. "I love you," he murmured softly, offering the only comfort he thought she would accept.

She shook her head, the sapphire depths of her eyes reflecting a bleakness more painful than the most agonizing scream. "How can I believe that?" she whispered. "I was watching you downstairs. You knew the history of the Shower. I don't believe you're here to buy it at all." The faint inflection at the end of her statement invited his confidence.

Involuntarily James took three steps toward her, stopping only when she put out her hand to warn him off. "I never said I was. I said I came to obtain the Shower," he corrected.

"You're not going to steal it?" Isis breathed, openly horrified at the prospect.

James grimaced at her conclusion. "No," he denied flatly. "Trade it, I hope."

"You're crazy," Isis pronounced, horror giving way to incredulous amazement. "Buffy's not about to part with that heirloom. You heard her."

"Perhaps." Catching Isis off guard, he closed the remaining distance between them. He grasped her arms before she had a chance to pull away. "Forget about the necklace. It has no bearing on us anymore."

Isis tipped back her head to stare at him. "How can you say that when that's the only reason we met?" She had to remember how they had come together, why they were here. She didn't dare allow her senses to react to him. She would not inhale the scent of him. She would not succumb to the temptation of his warm strength and let him hold her. He had lied.

"Let me go. I won't let you sweet-talk me into bed." The challenge slipped out before she could stop it.

James's eyes gleamed at the gauntlet thrown down before him. "Never sweet talk," he rasped, drawing her closer in spite of her attempt to escape. "My feelings for you are as real as you are. Don't you think I've felt guilty over my initial deception? If you walked out that door right now, who would know of our time together? Only you and I." He answered his own question before she could. "That's why I've never stayed at your home. After that first time in your room, I realized the danger. I wanted to protect you as much as I could if you came out of this hating me. I didn't want you to lie alone in a bed we shared remembering what was. I wanted your haven to be free of memories, so if you needed it it would be there for you."

Isis heard him out in silence, partly because he gave her no chance to speak, but also because his obvious honesty had damned up any rebuttal she might make. "I don't know, James," she admitted finally, the tension flowing out of her. In its wake, confusion reigned. Like a child's kaleidoscope, her emotions were shifting with each new revelation. He loved her, but he lied to her. He asked her trust, but offered her none about his reasons for seeking her out. He protected her, yet he used her acquaintance with the Metcalfs to gain entry into this house. He worked for another woman, yet his actions on most levels held a commitment to only her. Her heart and her body yearned for him and the passion he fired in her. Yet her mind couldn't accept what he had done and was still doing.

"I want to believe you."

James searched her eyes, the mirrors of her chaotic thoughts. He could almost touch the conflict going on within her. He drew her to him, wrapping his arms around her unresisting body. He inhaled deeply as she laid her head against his chest. At least she wasn't actively fighting him.

"I know you do," he sighed. He leaned his cheek against her hair, catching the jasmine scent that clung to the inky tendrils. Desire rose within him, but he tamped it down. He would be satisfied with this much for now. He had demanded enough of his woman. Her pain and confusion deserved his consideration. He would not force her beyond what she could and would freely give.

"I'll sleep on this damned chair-bed thing," he offered quietly, trying to disguise his dislike but not succeeding.

Isis lifted her head from its resting place to stare at the disputed furniture. She had heard his reluctance and the masculine disgust in his tone. "It's more my length than yours," she murmured after a short pause. "I'll sleep on it."

"No. You need your rest. Josie'll wring my neck if I take you home looking as tired as you did a week ago." He released her slowly when she leaned back in his arms to gaze at him.

"I'll be able to sleep just fine."

James's jaw clenched in annoyance at her stubbornness. "This is ridiculous. First you want me out of your bed. I'm out. I offer to sleep on this elegant torture rack so you can rest in solitary splendor and now you want me to take that bed." He glared at her.

She glared right back at him. "You won't be a martyr for my sake," she decreed, frustrated at his attitude. Any fool could see he was going to be uncomfortable on the chaise. It was barely long enough to accommodate her.

"Martyr!" he all but roared, remembering just in time to modulate his irritated exclamation.

"Yes, martyr," she agreed with a snap of her head. She turned away, kicked off her heels and collected her nightgown and robe. She stalked into the bathroom, slamming the door behind her.

James stared at the closed panel, his expression reflecting his temper. As the seconds passed a slow grin quirked his lips. His woman had the regal fire of an embattled queen when she got angry. What a life they were going to have once he got his present situation squared away. Absently changing out of his clothes into the pajamas bottoms he had brought just in case, he contemplated the bed problem. It was a foregone conclusion Isis wasn't about to give in and let him sleep on the chaise. And he wasn't risking a night of sleep for her when she was still replenishing her depleted physical reserves from the lengthy tour. Impasse.

The bathroom door opened with a muted click before he had a chance to find a solution. His eyes met hers, reading in them the same conclusion.

"Neither one of us is going to give in, right?" she murmured.

"No."

She glanced at the bed. "You stay on your side and I'll stay on mine?"

"Okay," he agreed carefully, stifling a chuckle at her fierce expression. Fleetingly he wondered which of them she was warning, herself or him.

Neither spoke as they slipped into bed from opposite sides. James switched out the lights to plunge the room into velvety darkness. Minutes ticked by measured by twin melodies of even breathing.

Isis lay without moving, more aware of James's body beside her with each passing heartbeat. It would be so easy to roll toward him and lay her head on his shoulder. She clenched her hands, feeling her nails score her palms.

"Relax, Isis. I promised I wouldn't encroach."

Isis started as his deep voice reached out of the silence to enfold her. "I know," she breathed, suddenly realizing how her attempt to curb her responses would have seemed to him.

"It's not easy for me, either. I lie here and all I can remember is the feel of you in my arms, the way you cry my name when I love you." He turned to face her, being careful not to touch her.

Isis gasped faintly at the images his words created. Heat flowed through her, reminding her of all they had shared. For one moment she savored the intensity of her reaction before she disciplined her wayward senses.

"Good night, James," she said firmly. His disgruntled sigh brought a slight smile to her lips as he echoed her words. Somehow the small exchange relaxed her more than she would have believed possible. Her lashes drifted slowly shut as the deep cadence of his breathing lulled her to sleep.

Isis came awake slowly to the sound of a rhythmic throbbing in her ear. Barely alert, she reached out a hand to silence the noisy thing interrupting her rest. Her fingers entangled in a soft rasp of hair on the too solid, too warm pillow beneath her head.

"Touch but don't pull," James admonished as she unconsciously stroked the rich pelt.

Isis snatched her hand away and jerked erect in the bed. "You said you'd stay on your half," she accused, coming awake with indecent rapidity.

James pillowed his arms behind his neck as he surveyed her, his eyes gleaming with humor and something more. "If you look at where *you* are and quit glaring at me like an enraged sphinx, you'd see *I* kept *my* word."

Every emphasized pronoun penetrated Isis's mind with stunning clarity. She glanced around, suddenly aware of the wide expanse of unoccupied bed on her other side. She shut her lashes against the undeniable evidence of her nocturnal poaching.

"Damn," she muttered. She felt rather than heard James's chuckle as he shifted positions slightly. He brushed against her lightly, reminding her of how little either of them wore in the snug warmth of their resting place. She scooted over, wondering whether jumping out of bed was any worse than the embarrassment of her current position.

"If you could see your face," James teased before dropping a brief kiss on her elbow. He felt her tremble at the tiny caress even as she pulled away.

"I wish you'd be quiet or get up or something," she grumbled, edging unobtrusively, she hoped, closer to her own territory. Blast him for being so obnoxiously cheerful. It was bad enough that it was barely light and she had chased him across the mattress while she slept, but was it really necessary he find her behavior so funny?

"How about the 'or something'?" he asked, knowing he was baiting her but unable to help himself. He had to play it light, otherwise he would never let her out of his arms or their bed. Just the sight of her disheveled beauty was doing unmentionable things to his libido. And that didn't count the restless night he had spent torn between cuddling the silky body that had insisted on clinging to him like a second skin or arousing the sleeping passion of his woman.

Isis's eyes snapped open at that, her back going rigid in protest to the tide of desire filling her. "You know what I mean," she countered swiftly. She tossed back the covers, aware that if she didn't get up now she never would. She bounced out of bed, half expecting James to try to stop her.

When he didn't, she hesitated a moment, her eyes going back to his as if drawn by a magnet. The tender heat in his fog-colored gaze poured over her, stealing her temper. Her lips twitched reluctantly in response to his slow, crooked grin. He looked so impossibly good lying there. His mussed hair and early morning stubble were more appealing than she wanted to admit. While his body.... She pulled her wayward thoughts back in line. She couldn't risk this now, she reminded herself sternly.

"Don't shut me out, Isis," James whispered, his smile dying with her mood change. "I know you can't fully trust me and I understand why. I haven't taken advantage of you and I won't. But must we act like strangers?" He paused, giving her time to answer. Would she relax just a little? One smile, freely given, wasn't too much to ask, was it?

Isis shook her head, recognizing his plea but unable to offer him or herself any solace. She wanted what they had shared back as much as if not more than he seemed to. For the first time in her life, she was afraid, afraid to risk any more of her heart than she had already. It was taking everything she had just to get through this weekend after knowing how he had manipulated her.

"Well?" he prompted when she remained silent. He stared into her eyes, trying to decipher the emotions swirling in the lake-blue depths.

"We could never be strangers. It might be better for both of us if we could be," she murmured finally, truthfully. She spread her hands in a gesture conveying her inadequacy at giving him a reply.

James sighed, annoyed with himself for beginning this tack. There was nothing he could accomplish without the explanations Isis deserved. And until Nora and Buffy met, thrashed out their differences and settled the fate of the Sapphire Shower, he could offer Isis no words to temper her belief in him.

"You can have the bathroom first," he suggested. "We don't have much time before we're due downstairs."

Accepting his choice of a neutral topic, Isis nodded her agreement. She turned away to select an outfit for her coming interview, grateful that James had backed off for the moment. She had no illusions about the issue lying between, but at least for now she didn't have to face them.

They showered and dressed in silence, easily switching places in the bathroom as though they had done it a thousand times in the past. His socks were missing; she found them. There was a snarl in her hair that no amount of careful contorting could bring her close enough to reach. He brushed it out. Finally, they were ready.

Isis followed him to the door, nearly bumping into him when he halted without warning and turned to face her. He caught her chin between his fingers, tilted it up, giving her a swift view of his gravely intent expression as he captured her lips in one searing kiss.

The lightning attack breached her defenses, eliciting a fiery response beyond her control. Her arms slipped around his shoulder while her fingers speared into his hair as she arched against him. His mouth moved on hers in an urgent quest for possession. He nipped her lower lip in a demand for access to the honeyed sweetness of her mouth. In a heartbeat, he gained his prize as Isis gave and took with equal mindless ferocity.

Passion blazed between them, bringing memories of desire and secrets shared. For a long, timeless moment they savored their past, locked in the inferno of the present. Bodies straining to reach beyond physical bonds, they clung together.

An instant later Isis jerked back, mirroring James's action and his expression. She stared at him, drawing in deep breaths in an effort to combat the devastating effect his kiss had had.

"Whatever happens today, remember that I love you. My body wants you and I want you. Remember that while you're recalling what I've done."

A plea, a command and a truth spoken from the depths of a man's most buried needs. Isis heard him out with a sense of awe and an odd feeling of exhilaration. She lifted her hand as she took a step toward him. Words trembled on her lips. An assurance, a plea of her own. He wasn't sure, but she knew she wanted to tell him she understood. She never got the chance. James backed away.

"Go fix your lipstick," he directed, allowing her no opportunity to speak. "Buffy and Burt will be waiting for us downstairs." He turned from her, knowing he had to put some distance between them. She was a temptation he had to ignore. He closed the door behind him, shutting out the sight of her vulnerable eyes and kiss-swollen lips.

"Damn Nora and myself," he muttered as his strides ate up the length of the hall to the main stairway. Soon it would be over. Would she forgive him his part? She had to. He needed her too much to bear the emptiness of his life without her.

Thirteen

Finally we can get started. I didn't think Burt would ever leave," Buffy remarked, settling back in her chair with an expectant look.

Isis smiled, vaguely surprised at how easy it was to be natural after the scene with James in the bedroom. When she had come down earlier, she had been prepared for some strain to exist between them. She couldn't have been more wrong. James had been in the harmless, casually friendly guise that was so much a part of him when they weren't alone together. Odd how he seemed to fade into the background when he was in public, she mused, momentarily forgetting Buffy's presence. A faint, polite cough from her companion recalled her before she could examine his behavior more closely.

"What should I do first?" Buffy asked eagerly when Isis glanced her way.

"Calm your mind," she answered, concentrating on the task before her. James and their situation would have to wait for a while longer.

Buffy tipped her head, a confused expression on her face. "How do I do that? Besides, I thought what happens just happens."

"Sometimes it does, but more often you have to prepare yourself and your mind to receive information," Isis explained, drawing from her own experience. "Remember we are working with a relatively unexplored form of communication. And this, like other methods of information transfer, depends on the strength of the message from the sender and the receptivity of the receiver. A radio station can send out the strongest signal in the world, but if no one has his radio on then no words are moved from the source to the listener."

"I think I get it," Buffy murmured thoughtfully. "So how do I clear my mind?"

Isis studied her silently, noting the suppressed energy vibrating in the older woman. "First you physically relax, let your mind float free."

She leaned back in her chair, demonstrating the position that worked best for her. Buffy copied her actions while carefully absorbing each of Isis's suggestions. Isis led her through a basic relaxation technique, while showing her how to concentrate on a pleasing, restful scene in her mind. Once Buffy's slow, even breathing confirmed her prepared state, Isis explained how to focus on a certain subject, how to tune out any distracting images. Minutes ticked by unheeded by either woman as Buffy repeatedly lost her calm and had to start from the beginning.

"I can't do it," she groaned in disgust, sitting up in her chair. A frown marred her usually cheerful features as she contemplated her teacher.

"It would be very unusual if you had succeeded this time. This kind of thing can take days or even years to develop if it happens for you at all," Isis pointed out honestly. "Every person is different. And more importantly, there are no set rules in this field. What works for me or another paranormal may not work for you."

"But I want to do this," Buffy countered with unexpected vehemence.

Isis opened her lips to ask why, just as Burt entered the room with a strange look on his face. What was up, she wondered, catching a fleeting impression of anger and deep concern. Isis's gaze focused on James as he followed the older man, searching his face for a clue to the suddenly fraught atmosphere. For a split second he met her eyes, his own containing a smoldering plea for forgiveness. Then with a blink an invisible shutter came down, wiping every trace of emotion from his features. Even as he walked toward her, he was watching Burt talk to Buffy.

"You did what?" Buffy demanded incredulously. Her eyes narrowed while her cheeks flared with angry color. "You know I won't have that woman in my house. Have you forgotten what her father did to mine?"

Shocked at the acid tones of Buffy's words, Isis stared at the other couple. Burt shook his head before reaching for his wife's hand. "I know you're upset, honey, but believe me, this is the only way."

Buffy snatched her fingers from his, glaring at him. "She's just after the Shower. You know that."

Isis felt James start to say something at the mention of the necklace. She turned her head slightly, wondering what his part was in all of this. The faint ringing of the doorbell was like an arctic blast, freezing them in place and stilling Burt and Buffy's argument. Anger pulsated in the silence as everyone stared at the door expectantly. A moment later a petite woman followed by a slim, silver-haired man appeared on the threshold.

"Mr. and Mrs. Harris," Soames announced, supremely unaffected by the emotion-filled quiet. Having done his duty, he retreated, his receding footsteps echoing loudly in the hallway.

"If you had any decency at all, you'd never have come here, Nora," Buffy bit out, rising agitatedly to her feet to glower at her uninvited visitors.

The woman Buffy addressed as Nora moved toward her quickly, her expression a mixture of distress and determination. "Buffy, I had to come. There's so little time left and I wanted to put things right between our families," she entreated.

Isis watched the scene unfolding before her in disbelief. This was Nora, the female James was shielding? She had to be close to sixty. A dozen questions came to mind but she asked none of them. This scene belonged to Buffy and Nora. She had no part in it. At the moment she was only a silent spectator.

"There's no need to be rude," Burt admonished carefully, going to Buffy's side. "Can't we all sit down and discuss this?"

"Rude?" Buffy expostulated furiously. She fixed her husband with a demanding look. "Just what has gotten into you?"

Burt shrugged uneasily, casting James a brief, unreadable look. "There's something you don't understand," he began when James only stared unhelpfully back at him. "The Sapphire Shower is stolen."

Buffy gazed at her spouse, her eyes wide with disbelief. "It can't be. You told me you bought it." She shook her head, backing away. "It's her doing. She's lying to you. It's mine."

Burt reached out to take her in his arms, but she slipped out of his grasp. "It's the truth, Buffy. I got the necklace from a fence who knew its history."

"Lies," she exclaimed wildly, whirling around to head for the door.

All through the emotional storm Isis had sat unmoving, listening and watching until Buffy bolted. Then, realizing none of them apparently knew how to stop her, she spoke. "It's no lie, Buffy," she stated, putting every ounce of confidence she possessed into her tone.

Buffy halted, turning slowly to stare at her. For a long moment during which no one made a sound she weighed her words. "You're sure?"

Isis nodded, never taking her eyes from her worried face. "I am." She patted the cushion on the chair beside her. "Come back and listen to what they have to say." She felt the tension in the room increase at her command. It was as if every breath was suspended awaiting Buffy's decision.

Slowly, drawn by Isis's calm assurance in the midst of the traumatic scene, Buffy walked toward her. "You'll read them for me?" she asked. "You'll tell me if they lie?"

"I will," she answered, perjuring herself without compunction. There was no way she could be as accurate at detecting an untruth as Buffy believed, but she suddenly realized she trusted James completely. He had brought these two women together for a reason. He had kept a confidence even when his silence had threatened their love. She believed in him in spite of everything.

Buffy sat down, her hands gripped tightly in her lap. "Okay, I'm waiting."

James stepped forward, gesturing for the packet Nora's husband held. "About eight months ago, Nora approached me to find a certain necklace taken during a robbery of her New York apartment. At that time she explained the history of the heirloom, and also the existence of a similar piece she and her husband had commissioned on the basis of an old letter written by your grandfather." He handed the bulky manila envelope to Buffy. "My job was first to find the Sapphire Shower if I could, and then I was to approach you on Nora's behalf to set up a meeting to resolve the family situation between you. Neither of us expected the assignments to overlap." He paused, glancing at Burt.

Reading the significance of his look, Burt picked up the story. "I entered the picture when I was contacted about buying the Shower. I knew it was stolen, but I also knew the story behind the fight over ownership and how much you wanted it. So I bought it."

Buffy fingered the package she held. "So, what now? I assume you've come to take the Shower back," she remarked bitterly, staring at her cousin.

Nora shook her head. "Not exactly. I've really come to exchange the Shower for this." She reached inside her handbag to withdraw a wide, slim jeweler's box. She snapped open the lid to display a necklace of silver, diamonds and sapphires closely resembling the disputed antique. "This is the Blue Cascade." She held it out to Buffy.

Buffy eyed the exquisite creation as though it were a serpent. "Why?" she demanded, making no move to accept the gems.

Nora swayed slightly, her face paling at Buffy's harsh tone. Instantly her husband was at her side to help her to the chair across from Buffy. "I'm dying, Buffy, and I want to set things right between us," she admitted starkly. She held up her hand in a silencing gesture when Buffy would have interrupted. "The envelope you have contains copies of letters and instructions to substantiate all I'm about to explain." She paused, seemingly gathering strength to continue. No one moved as they waited for her next words.

"About a year ago when I first discovered my condition, I decided I needed something to keep me busy and not brooding. I've always wanted to research our family's history so I set about digging in the past. During my search, I found grandfather's old diary. I found the entry of our fathers' births and their deaths. But what was more surprising, I also discovered the truth of the story about the Shower.

"Grandfather loved both our fathers dearly, but he always felt more rapport with your father than mine. So, even though my father was the older twin and the one grandmother had wanted to have her necklace, grandfather gave it to your father.

"Naturally, mine was hurt and jealous. But he was also realistic. Your father was known for his bad business sense, so he waited until the moment was right and offered to buy the Shower."

"He ruined him, you mean," Buffy interrupted fiercely.

"Possibly," Nora admitted, meeting her eyes steadily, "although I haven't found anything to prove he did contribute to your family's downfall.'' She paused, marshaling her reserves to continue. ''Having what he called his birthright never really brought him any satisfaction. He, in his own way, was probably just as bitter and hurt as your father. Anyway, when both of them died so young without ever speaking to each other again, our grandfather, unknown to us, decided to try and set things right. He commissioned a second necklace to be made, but he too passed away before all of the matched stones needed for the design could be collected. His plans were lost and the unset gems were passed on to me. Until a few months ago they were a matching bracelet to the Shower.''

She glanced down at the sparkling necklace she held. ''This is his gift as he wanted it created. The only difference is that I'm the messenger,'' she stated softly, almost meditatively, without raising her gaze. ''In the envelope you have is a letter he wrote just before he died. Will you read it now?''

Isis turned to the woman beside her, awaiting Buffy's reaction to the soft-voiced plea. Her attention, like the men's, had been riveted on Nora throughout most of her explanation. She read the indecision on Buffy's face as she fingered the packet she held.

''I don't know,'' she whispered, glancing first at her husband, then at Isis for guidance. ''Is she telling the truth or is this some kind of crazy trick to get the Shower back?''

''Look here...'' Nora's husband began in an automatic protest. It was the first time he had spoken since he had entered the room. Nora touched his arm, silencing him with the gentle gesture.

In the small diversion, Isis looked toward James. She caught his flash of anger at Buffy's slur and the quick restraint he exercised over his wish to protect his frail friend. He met her eyes, his face smoothed of all expression. But nothing hid the reassurance he offered her in the fog-colored depths.

"It's the truth," she stated simply as she faced Buffy once more.

With that Buffy nodded and opened the envelope to withdraw a paper yellowed with age. No one spoke or moved as she slowly read the message her grandfather had left for her. Tears welled in her eyes while she choked back a sob when she came to the end. She raised her head to stare at her cousin.

"Burt, would you bring the Shower?" she whispered, her voice thick with suppressed emotion. "So many years."

"I know," Nora agreed, her own eyes suspiciously bright. "And the terrible part was that grandfather never meant to hurt either of them."

Buffy sniffled inelegantly before surging to her feet. "Damn, I'm going to cry all over you," she muttered, throwing her arms around her relative in a fierce hug.

Nora received her readily as the necklace, forgotten by both, tumbled out of her lap to the floor. At that moment, Burt returned carrying the Shower. James, with Nora's husband at his side, moved to intercept him.

Feeling decidedly out of place, Isis eased out of her chair, being careful not to disturb the tender reconciliation. Keeping an eye on James in case he looked around, she made her way to the door and slipped out. She climbed the stairs, aware of a deep sense of relief. Everything that had troubled her about how and why she and James had met seemed so silly in the face of all she had learned. She realized now why he had been unable to confide in her. In an odd way, she even admired him for keeping his word.

But now what, she wondered as she entered their bedroom. Obviously, James was needed downstairs and probably still would be for a time yet, while she was definitely in the way. She was neither a friend of long standing nor a relative. She walked to the closet, having no clear idea of what to do. She disliked the idea of staying. Buffy and Nora were bound to have questions, maybe even disagreements to iron out once the initial emotional outpouring was over. A third party would surely complicate things.

She pulled out her suitcase and began packing. She would go downstairs and tell James she was going home and why. He would understand. Then when he was finished here, he could rent a car to drive up to Crystal Bay.

Feeling satisfied with her reasoning, Isis snapped the lock on her case a few moments later. After taking one last look around the room to be sure she hadn't forgotten anything, she walked out. There was no one in the hall when she reached the closed study door. She hesitated, her hand on the knob as the sound of raised voices penetrated the thick panel. She could make out Buffy and Nora with an occasional insertion by both husbands.

The quieting influence of James's comments rose and fell with each threatened argument. Unwilling to disturb him, Isis retreated to the chair placed a short distance away. Maybe if she bided her time James would come out, or the confrontation going on inside would ease enough for her to interrupt. Minutes ticked by with no change. Finally, realizing it was getting late, she decided to seek out Soames and give him the excuse for leaving she had concocted for the Metcalfs' benefit. She found him in the dining room.

"I've just been speaking to my housekeeper," Isis began without preamble. "My agent is flying in this evening with a contract problem. I'll need to drive back. Would you explain to the Metcalfs for me?"

The older man nodded aloofly. "As you wish," he murmured. He glanced past her to the closed den door they both could see. He was silent for a second as he studied her, then he inclined his head in a faint nod. A flicker of gratitude for her tactic showed in his eyes. "They will be sorry to see you go, but I'm sure they'll understand." He gestured toward her two cases waiting in the hall. "May I help you with those?"

Isis was startled into smiling at the unexpected offer from this very proper butler. "I'd like that," she agreed.

In less time than it had taken her to pack, she was on the road. She sighed as she relaxed behind the wheel, her gaze enjoying the beautiful scenery around her. Soon James would be joining her, and finally there would be no more barriers between them.

She hoped he wouldn't betray her small social fib, since he knew very well her agent was currently on vacation in the Bahamas. She shrugged, dismissing the possibility. He was too smart for that. He'd say all the right things, using that deceptive charm of his to the best possible advantage.

At one time his ability to blend in, to manipulate certain events, would have bothered her, but not now. She finally had the measure of the man she had chosen to love. She trusted him and she believed in his integrity. Hadn't his strength of purpose in helping Nora and his unfailing refusal to break his word even at the price of his own suffering shown her what he was?

It was late afternoon by the time Isis pulled into her driveway. The absence of Ned's station wagon indicated he and Josie had already gone in to Crystal Bay for their usual Saturday night casino outing. She slipped out of the car, stretching to ease the kinks from her body before extracting her cases. She glanced up at her house, enjoying the soft glow the slowly setting sun cast over the glass-and-wood design.

Flashes of colors reflecting off the stained-glass windows on the bottom floor welcomed her with a rainbow spectrum. With James here to share this with her, her life would be complete, she mused as she entered. She mounted the stairs, suddenly aware that she hadn't the least idea where he lived.

But no matter. Now they had all the time in the world to iron out the insignificant little differences. The important thing was she loved him and he loved her.

Night descended with no word from James. Isis lit a fire in the living room and settled down on the soft fur rug before the fireplace. She was a little disappointed in not having heard from him, but she hadn't really expected to.

She swirled her brandy in its snifter as she stared into the flames. He had his hands full. He would come to her when he could, she consoled herself. She leaned back against the jewel-bright pillows she had tossed down on the hearth. Her caftan flowed around her in a midnight-blue-and-silver river of silk. She sipped her drink, savoring the rich taste of the aged cognac on her tongue. The fire crackled softly, sending miniature showers of sparks over the logs.

The sound of a fast-approaching car disturbed the quiet, bringing Isis out of her contented position with a snap. She listened for the familiar purr of Ned's car. But it wasn't his.

James! As quickly as the name flashed across her mind, she was on her feet, the dark silk fluttering around her like raven's wings. She rushed to the foyer, her lips curving in a delighted smile of welcome. She paused just long enough to peer out the small window in the door to be sure it was him. Then she threw open the panel with a flourish to dash barefoot out onto the porch.

"James!" she greeted him eagerly as he stomped up the front steps. Her eyes took in the rugged sheepskin jacket he wore, the soft cloud of air that emerged with each breath. "You look cold."

"Cold?" James shot back, sweeping her up into his arms with one smooth motion. "You crazy woman, I'm too damned furious to be cold. What the devil are you doing, running out here like that? I could have been anybody. The least you could have done is put on some shoes." He stalked in the house, kicking the door shut behind him.

Shocked by his greeting, Isis stared up at his taut face. "But James," she began, trying to explain.

"Don't 'but James' me, Isis O'Shea," he growled, dropping her none too gently onto the sofa. He snatched the afghan that lay on one corner and tucked it around her. When he was done, he stepped back to glare at her. "Now, woman, you're going to sit there and listen to me. I've had a long day, and finding you gone on some stupid excuse was just the icing on the cake."

Fourteen

———

But James—'' Isis tried once more to interrupt her irate lover. She wriggled her arms free from her mummy's cocoon.

''Be still,'' he all but roared, yanking the afghan up to her chin. He dropped down on the sofa beside her. ''You may not have a lick of sense about your physical well-being, but I do. You need looking after. And I'm just the man for the job.'' He raked his fingers through his hair, his mouth clamped tight as he inhaled deeply. ''Damn, that's not what I meant to say,'' he swore in self-disgust. He got restlessly to his feet to pace to the fireplace.

Isis watched him, her eyes wide with surprise at his behavior. She had never seen him so out of control. He stared at the flames before him, unable to find the courage to turn around and face this woman he loved. ''I know I've hurt you about the way we met and how I used your connection with the Metcalfs to get into the estate," he explained, forcing the words out when all he really wanted was to hold her in his arms. "I kept telling myself Nora's need was greater, that you'd understand once everything was over." He swung around, too aware of the waiting silence. "You ran."

Isis caught the agony of his expression, realizing she was seeing his most vulnerable inner core as never before. The urge to take him in her arms had never been stronger. Yet the total stillness of his body stopped her. It was almost as if he were braced for a mortal blow. Every line, every muscle was taut as he confronted her.

"I didn't run," she said with quiet emphasis. "I came home to wait for you."

James stared at her, drinking in the sight of the calm serenity of her words. How he wanted to believe her. But could he? Could it be this simple? "Why?" he questioned hoarsely, his senses alert to every nuance.

Isis slipped out of her warm nest to rise to her feet. She unveiled the love she had in her heart, allowing it to warm her gaze as she walked toward him. "Because I love you," she whispered softly. She stopped before him, leaving only a fingertip of space between them.

James shook his head, his features tight with the emotions he was holding in check. "How can you? I lied to you. I approached you that first time, intending to gain your trust enough to convince you to accept Metcalf's invitation." He lifted his hand, surprised at the faint tremor he saw. "All I've done is take from you."

Isis covered his outstretched fingers with her own, a gentle smile curving her lips. "Are you trying to say you slept with me to get into my confidence?" His "no!" exploded at the same moment she added, "Because I won't believe you. You gave a gift of passion that first time, and with every moment we've shared you have renewed your present until there is no one else for me."

At her avowal, James relaxed completely. It was going to be all right. She didn't hate him. "If I could have any other woman in the world, I'd want no one but you, goddess," he confessed, pulling her close. His arms closed tightly around her, warming her with his own body heat. "You're in my heart and I couldn't get you out without killing myself."

Isis lifted her head from his shoulder, her arms sliding around his neck to pull him down to her level. "Be quiet and kiss me, lover, before we both expire of frustration," she groaned deeply.

James met her lips with a fierce hunger and possessiveness. His tongue surged deep in the sweet recesses of her mouth as he slowly drew her down onto the fur rug before the fire. What began as a wild surge of passion gentled into a beautifully sensual exchange of tenderness.

The firelight played around them as Isis curled into his hard body, cherishing the vulnerable part of him while challenging his essential strength.

"James," she breathed, her fingers deftly manipulating his coat off.

"Love me, Isis," he commanded, lifting his head for a moment to seek out the assurance he needed in her expressive eyes.

"Always." She touched his shirt lightly. "But I want to make love to you, too," she added, a wicked smile of ancient intent on her lips.

"Temptress," he rasped, taking her hint with indecent haste. Lovingly, he removed the caftan before divesting himself of his own clothes. He came down beside her to bury his face in her fragrantly scented hair before beginning a slow trail of kisses from her temple to the pulsating hollow in her throat. Feather-light caresses, all the more intoxicating for their restrained passion, rained over her heated skin.

Isis's tongue came out to trace a delicate pattern beneath his ear. Her hands glided over the sleek contours of his body tactilely loving every hollow and plane. Touch, caress, kiss, each exchange twisted their desire higher and tighter. She writhed beneath his sensual stroking, even as James trembled in her arms with the force of his own need.

His throaty growl echoed in the cavern of her mouth as he reclaimed her silken body for his own. Isis arched into his male strength, branding him with all the power of her femininity.

He was her lover, her seducer, her partner. He was the air she needed to survive. Her fingers roamed possessively over the moist skin of his back to grip his hips. She and James slipped the earthly shackles of time and space to soar together to a peak only they could see. Heat exploded around them in a dazzling display of fire and light.

With a cry, Isis gave in to the tempest, feeling James by her side through the storm. When it was done, she lay cradled in his arms, satiated and complete, fused now heart, mind and body.

James pressed her against his shoulder. When he felt the faint dampness on her face, he looked down at her with concern.

"Did I hurt you?" he asked softly, gently stroking the midnight curls back from her forehead. "When you make me go up in flames, I forget how fragile you are."

She smiled, loving the tender caring with which he always surrounded her. "I think these are another kind of tears." She closed her eyes, too drowsy to move.

James lowered his head and licked each droplet from her cheeks. No woman had ever given him so much. Her passion, her honesty, her understanding and her love were gifts beyond price. He meant to treasure every moment of the rest of their lives.

He cradled her closer to his body. "Marry me, love," he whispered against her ear.

Isis opened her eyes at the husky command. She searched his face. "It's not necessary—" she began slowly.

He interrupted. "It is. I want you and everyone else to know we belong to each other."

"What about our careers?" she asked, becoming more alert by the moment.

He smiled, his smoky eyes alight with secrets. "I have a plan all worked out," he whispered before he brushed her lips with a kiss meant to tantalize without fulfilling. "You'll have to marry me to find out what it is."

Isis's mouth bloomed beneath the provocative caress. "Now, that's an offer I can't refuse," she purred seductively before framing his face with her hands. "Even if it is blackmail."

"I can't believe I let you talk me into this," Isis stated as she unbuckled her seat belt. She leaned back in her chair while surveying her decidedly unrepentant husband with mock annoyance.

James grinned as he rose to go to the fully stocked bar at the rear of his Lear jet. "You're not trying to tell me you didn't enjoy your first assignment as my partner?'' He returned to his place carrying two brimming glasses of white wine.

Isis accepted her drink, unable to subdue a smile at his disbelieving tone. "To think that four months ago I was simply a night-club entertainer. Now I'm jetting around in a private plane." She glanced over the plush midnight-blue, silver and black decor before focusing on him once more. She raised her crystal glass in a salute. "Now I'm a sidekick to a recoverer of lost objects."

James returned her toast, his eyes gleaming with laughter and the deep love he had for her. "Partner," he corrected. "I never would have been able to flush Myerson out in the open if you hadn't picked up the location of those paintings. With his alibi and financial standing, he could have stayed with that story of the house fire destroying his collection forever."

"Luck." Isis shrugged, taking a sip of her wine.

"Talent and skill," he countered. He lifted her glass to place it on the table between them.

Isis's brow rose curiously at his suddenly intent expression. "James," she breathed softly as he framed her face with his hands.

"Do you really regret giving up the old ways?" he asked, his voice deep with his need for assurance.

Isis stared at him, tracing the features that had become as familiar to her as her own. "I regret nothing. You have given me a place where I truly belong. Your jet wings have given me travel. You've shared your work with me and that gives me a sense of purpose and adventure. Now I have two havens to return to when I'm tired, our house in Atlanta and the one in Crystal Bay."

She lifted her fingers to his lips. "But most of all, you've given me your love. I regret nothing for there is nothing I left behind."

For a long silent moment sapphire eyes met searching smoke-colored eyes. "You're a glorious creature, Isis O'Shea Leland," he murmured huskily as he covered her lips. His kiss held the strength of his love and the heat of desire she would always stir in him. His woman, his mate, his wife.

The Silhouette Cameo Tote Bag Now available for just $6.99

Handsomely designed in blue and bright pink, its stylish good looks make the Cameo Tote Bag an attractive accessory. The Cameo Tote Bag is big and roomy (13″ square), with reinforced handles and a snap-shut top. You can buy the Cameo Tote Bag for $6.99, plus $1.50 for postage and handling.

Send your name and address with check or money order for $6.99 (plus $1.50 postage and handling), a total of $8.49 to:

> **Silhouette Books**
> **120 Brighton Road**
> **P.O. Box 5084**
> **Clifton, NJ 07015-5084**
> **ATTN: Tote Bag**

SIL-T-1

The Silhouette Cameo Tote Bag can be purchased pre-paid only. No charges will be accepted. Please allow 4 to 6 weeks for delivery.

Arizona and N.Y. State Residents Please Add Sales Tax

Offer not available in Canada.

Silhouette Desire

COMING NEXT MONTH

A MUCH NEEDED HOLIDAY—Joan Hohl
Neither Kate nor Trace had believed in holiday magic until they
were brought together during the Christmas rush and discovered
the joy of the season together.

MOONLIGHT SERENADE—Laurel Evans
A small-town radio jazz program was just Emma's speed—until
New York executive Simon Eliot tried to get her to shift gears and
join him in the fast lane.

HERO AT LARGE—Aimée Martel
Writing about the Air Force Pararescue School was a difficult task,
and with Commandant Bob Logan watching her every move,
Leslie had a hard time keeping her mind on her work.

TEACHER'S PET—Ariel Berk
Cecily was a teacher who felt deeply about the value of an
education. Nick had achieved success using his wits. Despite their
differences could they learn the lesson of love?

HOOK, LINE AND SINKER—Elaine Camp
Roxie had caught herself an interview with expert angler
Sonny Austin by telling him she was a fishing pro. Now she was on
the hook to make good her claim.

LOVE BY PROXY—Diana Palmer
Amelia's debut as a belly dancer was less than auspicious. Rather
than dazzling her surprised audience with her jingling bangles, she
wound up losing her job, her head and her heart.

AVAILABLE NOW:

TANGLED WEB
Lass Small

HAWK'S FLIGHT
Annette Broadrick

TAKEN BY STORM
Laurien Blair

LOOK BEYOND TOMORROW
Sara Chance

A COLDHEARTED MAN
Lucy Gordon

NAUGHTY, BUT NICE
Jo Ann Algermissen